Music I Never Dreamed Of

John Gilgun

John ... ... from Jorkn- bay. Ap. 12, '94

Amethyst Press
New York, NY

This book is a work of fiction. Any similarity between persons, places, and things in this text and actual persons (living or dead), places, and things, is purely coincidental.

AN AMETHYST PRESS FIRST EDITION
COPYRIGHT © 1989 by JOHN GILGUN

Published in the United States of America by Amethyst Press, Inc. 462 Broadway, Suite 4000, New York, NY 10013

ALL RIGHTS RESERVED. No part of this book may be reproduced in any form without written permission from the author, except for brief passages included in a review appearing in a newspaper or magazine.

COVER ART BY CARLOS QUIROZ

Library of Congress Cataloging-in-Publication Data
Gilgun, John.
Music I never dreamed of / by John Gilgun.
p. cm.
ISBN 0-927200-02-3: $8.95
I. Title.
PS3557.I354M8 1990
813' .54—dc20
89-38385
CIP

2

FOR JERRY ROSCO
who believed in this book

1

I remember what it was like being twelve, thirteen, fourteen years old. Someone in the gang would say something or do something and the urge would come over you—we called it "being in the mood"—and you'd yell, "Bop bop!" Your friend would answer, "Bop bop de bop!"—And then you'd be on each other, wrestling, you know, down on the ground, tangled up in each other's arms, legs, clothing. Wrestling, yes, but going for the cock and balls too, because that was sexy and fun. Of course it was also a sin and you had to confess it on Saturday afternoon. We were good Catholic boys, Irish and Italian, and boppin' was a bad sin because it was sexy and sex was the worst sin. They had told us that and we believed it, but not enough to stop boppin'. We bopped all the time, confessed it on Saturday afternoons, took Communion on Sunday and then, Monday afternoon after school...Bop bop de bop!

Confession went like this:

"Father, I committed impure actions."

"With who?"

"With my friend."

"How often?"

"Three or four times."

"What did you do?"

"We wrestled around and touched each other."

"Through the clothing?"

"Yes, Father."

"Three 'Our Fathers' and two 'Hail Mary's.' Make a good Act of Contrition."

My Acts of Contrition were good. That is, I could convince myself I was sorry—until I turned from the altar and saw my friend

Vin waiting to walk me home. His name was Vin Romano, "Ro" for short, and he was a beautiful dark-haired Italian with clear skin and green eyes like a cat's. "Whadja tell Father Dolan?" he'd ask.

"Impure thoughts, impure actions."

"Yeah, me too. What'd he give y'?"

"Three 'Our Fathers' and two 'Hail Mary's.'"

"Yeah. Me too."

And we knew we couldn't bop until after Mass next day because you had to be in a state of grace to take Communion. The period from Saturday night to Sunday morning was dangerous because you couldn't have a "sexy thought" either. If you saw one coming you had to ward it off, as you'd ward off an attacking dog with a stick. And Ro was always there, sitting beside me in the movies—our parents sent us to the movies every Saturday night— with his arm or his leg pressed up against me. His body was warm and he smelled of soap and Vitalis, but it was a sin to think about the flesh. If you went to Communion knowing you'd sinned, God was displeased and you were in danger of hellfire. You couldn't get the sin wiped away until the following Saturday, which made for a scary week.

We had debated the sinfulness of wet dreams and decided that since they were sexy, they must be sinful. One night I had one and it happened to be a Saturday night, which meant no Communion in the morning since I was no longer sinless. In this dream, Ro and I were naked as we bopped and there was a feeling of tenderness in it which I recognized as love. I called it that because that's what it was and I hadn't learned to lie about it yet. When I didn't go to the altar with the others for Communion, a cousin ratted on me to my mother and I had to face that when I got home.

"You didn't go to Communion," my mother said.

"How'd you know that?"

"Never mind. Are you in a state of grace?"

"Yes," I lied.

"Liar," she answered, and she slapped me.

"O.K. No, I'm not! I just lied. I'm angry as hell. There, I just swore! And I am not honoring my parent."

I was kept in for a week after school as a punishment for this. But at least I had gotten out of mentioning the wet dream. You couldn't talk to your mother about wet dreams. No way.

Ro discovered he could bop with girls, only then it was called "feeling 'em up." He was so good-looking, the girls came to him, when they could get away with it, to "fool around." Mostly this took place in the deep grass on the edge of the woods beyond the softball diamond. I began to see less and less of Ro, which bothered me. I disliked the girls, who seemed gross to me. They were soft where guys were lean. They shrieked and giggled and even cried sometimes—cried for no reason at all when you least expected it! They were all wrong somehow and yet, all of a sudden, they were part of my world and my friend—well, my friend was fascinated by them.

One Saturday afternoon after Confession, Ro said, "I had to tell Dolan I felt up Jackie Sverdlaka."

"That's no sin," I answered.

"What's no sin?"

"Feelin' up an animal. It's only a sin if it's a human being."

We walked on in silence. Then he said, "Jackie Sverdlaka's a human being."

I said, "She's a pig."

We walked some more. Then he said, "You shouldn't talk like that. The guys will call you 'homo'."

"Why?"

"Because you don't like girls. You call 'em pigs."

"Yeah, but you do, too. I heard you call 'em pigs hundreds of times."

"That's different."

"How 'different?'"

"I don't mean it. You really mean it. You hate 'em. It's gonna get you in trouble with the guys. Try to like girls even if you don't."

"But that don't make sense, Ro! How can I like something I don't like?"

"I don't know. But y' gotta try. Otherwise you're in trouble with the guys. Work on it, Valyo. Work on it."

"Valyo" was my nickname and meant "Valiant One." I had a reputation for never backing down from a dare. I was a skinny redheaded kid who wore glasses. And once, after a Retreat, I even said I wanted to be a priest. So I had to be valiant. I couldn't afford to back down. But now it got around that I didn't dare feel up Jackie Sverdlaka, so after a while the guys in my gang didn't call me "Valyo" any more. They didn't call me "homo" either. They didn't call me anything at all. For the guys who'd been part of my gang—Jack Parnell, Buckie Buchanan, Frank Chirichetti—I no longer existed. They all dropped away. Only Ro was left. And then one day he went, too. We were standing side by side in a city park and all of sudden he hit me across the face. No warning. He just hit me. My glasses flew off and landed in the grass. Then we were down on the ground and he was sitting on top of me screaming, "I'm not your friend no more! No more! You understand that? No more."

"You're still my friend," I said.

"Naw," he said, and he hit me in the face again. It was dirty fighting, hitting a guy in the face when you had him pinned down, but this was no ordinary fight. "And if you come around here again I'll tell everybody about you."

"Tell everybody what?"

He hit me again. "Are you gonna say, 'I won't come around?'"

"What about me?"

"Say it!"

"O.K. 'I won't come around.' But what about me? What?"

Ro stood up and walked away. He never spoke to me again.

He had bloodied my nose and the blood got all over my tee shirt. I put it with the other dirty clothes in the hamper. A few days later my mother confronted me with it. "Why is this shirt bloody?" she asked.

I had cried myself out after the fight. I had no tears left, I told myself. But then I could feel them coming again, so I shouted, "It's bloody because it's got blood on it. That's why it's bloody. Can't you see?"

She looked at my face and saw something there. Or maybe it was the absence of something there. "What's wrong?" she asked. "What's the matter with you?"

I said nothing. I just continued to stare at the blood on the shirt.

"You can tell me, Stevie. What is it? What's wrong?"

"Nothin' you can fix," I answered. Then I turned, went into my room and slammed the door behind me.

2

My mother had a procedure which she followed every working day of her life. First she put polish on her waitress shoes—Griffin Liquid White on Enna Jetticks. Then she ironed her uniform, the nylon dress, the cap with the scalloped edge that was like a fancy dinner napkin, the apron. Finally she did her nails, smoking a Walter Raleigh cigarette while they dried. She worked in the Governor Bradford Room of the Beaconsfield Hotel in Boston's Back Bay. Very plush. Seventy cents an hour plus tips in the early Fifties. She was ironing that morning when I walked into our kitchen in South Boston. I was nineteen years old and had just been washed out of Sacred Heart Seminary in Manchester, New Hampshire for "lack of vocation." I was ready to go to work myself now, bring some money into the house, accept responsibility, grow up, be a man, all the things she'd been telling me in her letters were so important. But she didn't look up when I came in, which meant that something was wrong.

"Well, I'm home," I said, dropping my duffle bag on the waxed linoleum. "Aren't you even going to say welcome home?"

"Welcome home," she said, with that irony I'd expected. Very Irish, that irony. And very Irish, too, the anger it didn't quite conceal. "The paper's on the table there, open to Help Wanted. I circled a couple of things for you. Start making your calls now. It's almost nine o'clock."

"Hey, gimme a break! Can't I even take my coat off first?"

"There are hundreds of men out there, men out of work, men with families to support. They're lined up out there."

"I'll get a job!"

"Damn right you'll get a job. They'll draft you now anyway, but till they do you'll hold down a job just like everyone else, Mister High and Mighty."

I took off my coat, the peacoat I'd bought the day before at an Army-Navy store in Manchester. The coat was part of my new image, along with the duffle bag, the knit cap, the red and black checkered lumberman's shirt and the lace-up boots. I wanted people to think I was a merchant seaman, a farmer, a factory worker, anything but an ex-seminarian. Still, my serious little face, my big eyes, my thin lips and my glasses, those round glasses in their clear plastic frames, seemed to say, unmistakably, to me anyway, "seminarian." I was self-conscious about the glasses, but since everything was a blur without them, what could I do? They'd fogged over as soon as I'd stepped into the hot, steamy kitchen, so I wiped them on my sleeve. As I put them back on my nose, a headline leaped up at me: McCARTHY TO EXPOSE NEW RED LINK TO ARMY. It was February, 1954, and Joe McCarthy was doing his little dance in Washington. But that had nothing to do with me.

Why was my mother angry? I wondered. She hadn't wanted me to go to the seminary in the first place, so why was she angry now that I'd left? The truth was, I hadn't wanted to go there myself, so how had I ended up there? Well, you go to parochial schools for twelve years, a priest visits your class during senior year, he singles out the guys with good grades, the ones who hand in their Latin homework on time, the ones who don't date much, and he says, "Have you considered Sacred Heart?" So you go. The first year is just an extension of high school, so you coast. Second year you're told, "You don't have a vocation," and you're bounced. That was the route I'd taken, drifting along, letting other people make my decisions for me. But no more. No more.

"Stevie," she said. "I don't care what kind of trouble you got into up there. That's all in the past. Just get a job. It's all forgotten."

"There wasn't any trouble. Father Cullen called me in and told me I didn't have a vocation, that's all."

"Yes, I know. That's how they do it. I don't want to talk about it."

"If you don't want to talk about it, why are you talking about it? I told you there wasn't any trouble and there wasn't any trouble. What do you think, that I stole something or what?"

13

They'd kicked a guy out just before Christmas for lifting wallets from lockers.

"No, you've never been a thief," she said, implying that I'd possibly been everything else. "One thing you've never been, Stevie, and that's a thief."

At that moment my older brother Brian came into the kitchen, dressed to go out. He worked at the Rexall drugstore on the corner and that's where he was going, to work. Well, everyone worked. That's what it was all about. Pretty soon I'd be working, too. Good. Brian looked at my mother and some message passed between them, though neither said a word. Then he turned to me and laughed, a nervous little laugh. "Hey, Stevie! Good to see you. Walk down to the drugstore with me. Take the paper. Make your calls from the pay phone. I want to talk to you on the way down."

As we went out, my mother said, "Brian, remember what I told you."

And he answered, "Yeah. Sure."

*

We lived a block from a spice warehouse and a Wonder Bread factory, so when the wind was right we used to say, "Whadda we got? Cinnamon toast!" It was a cinnamon toast morning, with the wind blowing in from the harbor, and that felt good, even though the cold was like a kick in the crotch. Getting out in the clear air was especially nice after being in that kitchen where, because the storm windows had been up since November, you could smell every potato that had been boiled in there in the past three months. Our flat was on the third floor of what they call a "three decker," and as we started down the open stairway leading to the backyard, walking slowly because of the icy steps, Brian said, "Ma thinks you got in trouble at the seminary."

"I know, I know. I just went through that. What kind of trouble?"

"She wouldn't tell me."

"I believe that. She never comes right out and says it. But she lets you know anyway. So what is it?"

Brian had had rheumatic fever as a kid and he had that bluish-white skin you see sometimes on people who have to watch their hearts. He turned red under that skin now and answered, "I think she thinks you're turning into some kind of radical, an atheist, something like that. You said something in a letter to her? Something you read in a book up there? I don't know. Ah, hell, Stevie, she's going through 'the change.' She imagines things. It's terrible, really terrible, living here with her now." Then, "I'm moving out. I'm getting married."

I wasn't surprised. Brian had been going with one girl, Mary Mangan, since the ninth grade. So it was now or never. How long can you ask a girl to wait? "Does Ma know?" I asked.

"No. I'm going to tell her tonight. Dad will be there. I'm picking him up at the hospital at five o'clock."

My father had a booze problem, very bad, very heavy. It was killing him and he didn't really care. But every few months he committed himself to a hospital run by his fraternal organization, The Sons of Erin, to dry out. He hadn't worked for a year, not since he lost his job with Cahill Cartage for being drunk while driving one of their delivery trucks. When Brian moved out, my mother would lose not only his company, which she had come to depend on, but the ten dollars a week he paid for room and board. But, she'd have me now, God help me!

We had reached the yard and were standing on cinders and rock salt beside the trash cans. "Hey, Stevie, you want to double date with me and Mary on Friday?" Brian asked. "Her cousin Theresa's visiting her from Providence. You can take her. We're going bowling."

This was something new. Brian had never asked me to double date with him before. Who wants the kid brother tagging along? I'd never met the cousin and probably wouldn't be able to think of anything to say to her, but Brian would be there to take up the slack if I clammed up. And then I knew, suddenly, without needing my proof, that my mother had put him up to this. I mean, I just knew. I looked at him. He caught my look and glanced away, even more embarrassed than he'd been before. But I said, "Sure. O.K. Great. I'll take her."

"Good. I'll tell Mary. Theresa's a nice girl. You'll like her."

Girls! When I was four years old I played house with the girls in the neighborhood. Once or twice I was the mother and put on a dress. That got knocked out of me fast. If you did things like that, you were a sissy, a pantywaist. You weren't supposed to have anything to do with girls at all apparently, so after a while I didn't. I worked at being "a real boy." But then, just about the time I began to get good at it, when I was about fourteen, you were supposed to like them again. Or anyway, you were supposed to enjoy chasing them and grabbing their tits. You could still act as if you didn't really like them when you were with the guys. You could still prefer to hang out with the gang. But you had to enjoy grabbing their tits.

15

If you didn't, you could be ridiculed in the same way you had been ten years earlier when you played house with them. And boppin' with guys—the thing that made you a tough little kid at fourteen, sexy and smart and rebellious—now meant you were a sissy again, or worse! And suddenly you were supposed to get laid. That wiped everything off the board and you could start over. What happened was, you found the right girl, you fell in love with each other, and then, when the moment was right, you got laid. Then you got married because that was the right thing to do. Or you waited till your wedding night, because you respected the girl. And all the waiting gave an edge to it, or so they claimed. Or you found a girl who put out and you lost your cherry, and that was something to brag about later with the guys, but you'd never marry a girl like that even though everybody knew that whores made the best wives. All I'd ever done though was to make out a couple of times on the steps of the high school during CYO dances. Making out meant kissing and it was something I did because it was expected of me, but kissing some girl I hardly knew on those cold, concrete steps in the dark with the statue of St. Patrick staring down from his pigeon niche up above, a girl who was usually bored or indifferent or frightened, left a lot to be desired in my opinion. Still, when you walked back inside and the guys saw you'd been outside on the steps making out, they respected you and treated you better. Of course I never told anyone how I really felt. Some night I'd find the right girl and everything would be all right. That's how it worked.

"Brian, do you...? Do you...?" I wanted to say, "Do you get laid?" But I couldn't say it. Brian would have had to lie. If he was getting laid, he'd have had to lie to protect Mary, who had to be a virgin when she put on that white dress to walk to the altar. And if he wasn't getting laid, he'd have to lie to protect himself, because he couldn't let me think he was still jacking off at the age of twenty-one, though of course he was, because what else could he do if he wasn't getting laid?

"Do I what?" he asked.

"Do you...? Do you believe in anything?"

"Sure," he answered. I believe in everything. What else is there?"

"Yeah. Ha!" I said, laughing. "Me too!"

I made my calls from the phone booth in the drugstore, looking out through the glass at my brother checking out customers at the cash register. I wasn't qualified for most of the jobs

16

and half of them required a car. But finally I scored. It was a job in a cafeteria, and since I'd worked with my mother as a busboy at the Governor Bradford Room a couple of times, I figured I was qualified. Food is food. I used the words "extensive restaurant experience" and that did the trick, because the voice on the other end of the line said, "Sure, come right over." So I made the "V for Victory" sign to Brian, who was really too busy to notice or respond. The place was mobbed—people buying Kleenex, cough drops, Vick's. It wasn't good for Brian to be working in there. With his heart condition, he shouldn't have been exposing himself to people with colds and flu. But what could he do? He had to work. I went outside to wait for a bus on the corner.

There were a lot of people out there too, all bundled up in their coats, looking like hibernating bears that have been jolted awake two months early and aren't all that happy about it. Every half-frozen face seemed to say, "I wish t' Christ I was home in bed!" And my old friend Ralph Ultrino, who had graduated from high school with me a year and a half before, was with them. "Hello, Valyo," he said. "When'd you get home?" Valyo! Nobody'd called me that in years! It made me feel good, like we shared something, memories, a mutual past.

"I got back this morning," I said. "I'm not going back. I'm looking for a job."

"You're not going to be a priest?"

"Ralph, I'd have made the world's worst priest," I said.

He was buried deep down inside a khaki colored army parka, the hood of which was drawn tight against his forehead. He had a scarf over his chin too, but even so, you could see... You could see that Ralph was very good-looking. You couldn't say it. You couldn't even think it, not really. But it was there. It registered on your consciousness. No way around it. I heard somebody say once, "Man, there are some good-lookin' Guineas in this world and Ralph is sure one helluva good-lookin' Guinea!" Who said it? Another Guinea, naturally. Italians could say things like that about other Italians, but if you weren't Italian, watch out!

We talked. What happened to Fucci? Collins? O'Brien? Didja hear Maureen Clancy married a Jew and her family won't speak to her? O'Hare and Luciano are in the army, in friggin' Korea, for crissake! The usual stuff. "And O'Bannion," Ralph said. "Remember Kevin O'Bannion? He's in Mass General for observation. Tried to kill himself. Slashed his wrists."

Sure I remembered O'Bannion. They called him "Come-head O'Bannion" because he had a streak of white running through his black curly hair. You'd see his name on the walls of toilets at school, because he was supposed to give blow jobs. Guys would yell at him on the way home from school, "O'Bannion owes for blows!" Then a bunch of them would jump him and beat him up. Picking on him started in grade school because that streak of white made him stand out. Of course I had a mop of red hair, so I stood out, too. But with red hair, you get a reputation for having a temper, so people think twice before they mess with you. But it could have been me with my glasses. And I did my homework too, got high grades, never got slapped around by the nuns, was always picked to play the lead in plays and pageants. But it was never me. It was always O'Bannion.

"Yeah," Ralph went on. "He went in the service, y' know, and he had a nervous breakdown, so they let him out. He came home and got a job in the chocolate factory, but he couldn't make it in civilian life either. I feel sorry for the guy. Nobody deserves that kind of pain."

Most guys wouldn't have risked that—expressing sympathy for somebody like O'Bannion, I mean—but Ralph wasn't like most guys. A couple of times, in school, he'd even stopped guys from beating up on O'Bannion. Ralph could go in there and say, "Hey, look! Don't do that." And the guys would quit. Ralph had the qualities of a good labor leader, the cool, smart kind that wears a suit and has an office with a secretary. Ralph wasn't a hood...well, I mean, he was a hood, but he was a gentleman hood. He had class. He had class and he had heart, the unbeatable combination.

"And I don't think O'Bannion did half those things the guys said he did," Ralph said. "He'd have had to blow every guy in town twice over if he'd done everything they said he did."

The crowd moved all at once, collectively, which meant the bus was coming. We were shoved forward by people behind us. Just as the bus pulled forward, it popped out of me. It was as if, having been unable to ask my brother if he was getting laid, I just had to ask this of Ralph. "Hey, Ralph, did O'Bannion ever make a pass at you?"

Everyone in the crowd must have heard me. Ralph turned bright red, though his face was already red from the cold. "Naw, whadda y' think? I'd have decked the fruit!"

That should have been it. But it was still on his mind, apparently, as we stood on the bus, jammed in there, bouncing back

18

and forth, but managing, even so, to keep our bodies from touching. "Madone!" he said, making a jerking motion with his head. "What a pair of knockers on that one!"

I looked but saw only a wall of papers in front of the people who'd been lucky enough to grab seats.

ARMY CHIEF TO TESTIFY
McCARTHY DEMANDS ARMY NAMES NOW
ZWICKER UNFIT FOR UNIFORM SAYS JOE

No knockers. Or anyway, none that I could see. But I answered, "Yeah, wow," because that was what you had to say. It was expected of you. Otherwise you might as well be O'Bannion.

Then Ralph relaxed and leaned against me. What else could he do on a crowded bus? But he must have thought, "What do I have to prove?" In his case, nothing! So he relaxed and leaned. And as we touched, something exciting passed between us. There was a surge, a charge. It reminded me of being a kid again, of horseplay, of wrestling around together in the grass, of being close, of boppin'. Did Ralph ever bop in junior high? No, he was always off to the side. He was indifferent. Or he was disdainful. He never joined in. I knew I wasn't supposed to feel good about remembering stuff like that. It came too close to being queer. Well, maybe it wasn't really queer unless you actually did something, made a pass or something, committed yourself to it physically, gave blow jobs. Anyway it was a phase. You outgrew it. You got laid and then it all cleared up, like acne. But I couldn't deny it. Being in contact with Ralph this way made me feel good.

"What was it like at Sacred Heart?" Ralph asked.

"Oh, you know, 'Hard bed, bad food, cold floor.' You know that joke?"

"No, how's it go?"

"Well, this woman wants to be a nun. So she goes to the convent and they put her in a cell and keep her there for ten years. Then they let her out and tell her she can speak two words. So she says, 'Hard bed.' So they put her back in the cell for ten years, let her out again and give her two more words. She says, 'Bad food.' Ten more years and they let her out and she says, 'Cold floor.' They're really pissed off at her, so they send her to the Mother Superior. And the Mother Superior says, 'We're gonna have to let you go. All you've done since you got here is bitch, bitch, bitch.'"

He chuckled. "It was like that. 'Hard bed, bad food, cold floor.'"

"Yeah?"

"Yeah, but that wasn't the real problem. I started to ask questions about religion, and you can't do things like that. It would have been O.K. if I'd kept the questions to myself, but I spoke up. The other guys were afraid of me. I made them nervous. Nobody dared speak to me. I was completely out of it up there. One thing led to another and here I am, looking for a job."

"What kind of job you looking for?" Ralph asked.

"I don't know. Anything. Any openings where you work?"

"What? At Pawtucket Paper Box? Sure, there's always openings there. But you don't want to work there!"

"Why not?"

"It's a terrible place. You'd hate it. You know, you should be in college, Valyo, at B.C. or Holy Cross or some place like that. You're smart. You don't want to waste your time making paper boxes."

"Well, at Sacred Heart, Ralph, for the last couple of months, every time I'd crack a book I'd get sick to my stomach. I'm not just saying that. I'd really get sick."

"No shit?"

"I wouldn't lie to you, Ralph."

He was practically on top of me. He was chewing some kind of peppermint gum. His scarf was down below his chin and his mouth was moving. I was staring at his lips. The peppermint smelled so good. All at once I got caught up in the peppermint smell. I got carried away too by his body bumping against mine. Even through all that clothing I could feel it. Then I passed right out of myself and into Ralph. It was weird but nice. For a second I was Ralph, in his body, looking out at the world through his eyes, and it was a good world, rich and full of possibilities. But it was more than that. I sensed the world through Ralph's skin, his bones, his belly, his legs. And my body responded. Well, you outgrew stuff like this. But I couldn't ignore the voice in my head that said, "But it's great, so why bother!" That was the voice you had to repress. Ralph moved away. He was getting off here. Before he left though, he said, "Hey, I'll see what I can do. I'll talk to my foreman. Like I said, there's always openings. I'll call you tonight and let you know. Hey, and…don't let the bastards grind you down, O.K.?"

*

Ah, the Fifties! When I think back on it, I hear a million and a half toilets flushing at the same time all over Eastern Massachusetts, from Ipswich to Bridgewater, from Hull to Concord, at sixteen minutes past eight every Tuesday night. An official with the

20

state water conservation board noticed that the water level in the big reservoir out in the central part of the state dropped a few inches every Tuesday night at sixteen minutes past eight, and he figured out that a million and a half people got up from their chairs when the second Texaco commercial came on during the Milton Berle show and went into their bathrooms to take a leak. When they all flushed, the water level dropped. His discovery made all the papers. Maybe it should have made me feel close to all these people, who were only doing what human beings have to do, but it didn't. Maybe it was because they were doing it *en masse,* I don't know. Anyway, it didn't take long for the politicians to figure out that if people could all piss at the same time, they could all think the same thoughts at the same time too. That's where television came in. And anyone who still dared to think his own thoughts, well, that's what Joe McCarthy was all about. You could be punished for it. You could be dragged in front of a committee. You could be asked, "Are you still having your own thoughts?" You could lose your job. And then you'd never get hired again. You'd be ruined.

Since it was Tuesday night, there we were, my mother, my father, my brother, myself, sitting in our parlor in front of the nine inch Emerson, waiting for Uncle Miltie to come on, just like everybody else in America at that moment. The papers were praising television for "bringing the American family together again." What a joke! Consider my family. My mother had worked a big banquet that day, coming home at four o'clock almost hysterical because her boss, a Greek named Nick, had "insulted her." The Governor Bradford Room, for all its pictures of Squanto and the Mayflower and wild turkeys and Plymouth Rock, and in spite of its Indian pudding and cranberry relish, was run by a gang of Greek investors, a kind of Thessalonian Mafia. Anyway, she came home, locked herself in the bathroom and cried. I had come in about three. No, I hadn't gotten a job. I'd been told by one personnel manager after another, "no experience, no job." The old double bind. That lie about "extensive restaurant experience" got me nowhere. I had no references. I couldn't even give the name of one single maitre d'. So they knew I was lying. But I wasn't discouraged. It was all new to me and I sort of enjoyed it. I was meeting a lot of new people, every personnel office was different, I was learning things and there was always the chance I'd get something. In that way it was like gambling. It was fun. I liked it. I told my mother, "I think I got something," because that's what she wanted to hear, and I definitely would get something too, maybe tomorrow. About six o'clock Brian brought my father in. "I need peace and quiet," my father said. Fond hope! His nerves were as ragged as the end of a rope, because that's what the drying out process did to him, but he'd come to the wrong place if he wanted to relax. And Brian was going to have to tell my mother that he was getting married and moving out. He couldn't do it, though. All through supper he kept trying. I'd see him start to say it, but then, no... He couldn't. He just couldn't. He'd look up from the mashed potatoes and peas and he'd really try but nothing would come out. It was painful to watch him. At eight o'clock we ran for the television, thinking it would numb our pain. It didn't, of course. We needed something stronger than that. Like morphine maybe!

Berle came on, the most popular man in America at that time, with something like a hundred million Americans watching him. He came on, dressed as a fairy godmother in a ballgown, wearing a wig with a tiara on top of it and carrying a wand. And he said the same things he said every Tuesday night. "I know there's an audience out there. I can hear somebody breathing." "No applause, please. No applause. More more more!" "I'll kill you. I'll kill you a million times." And finally, "Make-up!" Then a funny looking guy ran out as he did every week and swatted him across the face with a big powder puff. "I think there must be fairies at the bottom of your garden!" Berle said, hitting the guy with his wand.

Brian leaned forward and turned the channel. "I've had enough of that fairy," he said.

"Hey!" my mother said.

"I'm sick of Berle," my brother said. "It's the same every week."

"Hey, I like him," my mother said.

"Shut up," my father said. "Can't a man get any peace?"

"Turn it back," my mother said.

"No," Brian said. "Let's watch something different for once!"

Then Bishop Fulton J. Sheen materialized on the screen, waving his arms, twirling his cape, his eyes glinting in a maniacal way, a crazy grin flickering across his face. He looked like some contemporary manifestation of The Devil, which was ironic, because he was a priest! Talking rapidly, he drew a wheel on the blackboard. We heard him say, "God is the hub and we are the spokes. The nearer we come to God, the closer we come to each other." Then the camera was no longer on the blackboard. It was on Sheen. Bells rang. Sheen did something funny with his cape. Then they let you see the blackboard again and presto, the wheel had been erased. Sheen threw his arms out, agitating his cape, and said, "My angel erased it." His eyes were so bright, so glazed—like pearl onions simmering in a stew.

Then it popped out of me. I don't know where it came from. I guess I just couldn't help myself. "I think there must be fairies in the bottom of his garden, too," I said.

There was a feeling of terrible tension in the room all of a sudden. Then my mother said, "You can't say things like that! That man's a priest!"

"It's O.K.," I answered. "It's television. He can't hear me."

"Oh, you have such a smart mouth!" my mother cried, and she slapped me across the face. My glasses flew off somewhere and everything blurred in front of me. Then she slapped me a second time, saying, "That's just the kind of thing you'd say. Only you could come up with something like that."

Brian got between us. "Hey! Leave the kid alone, Ma! Can't you leave the kid alone? Can't you quit this now?"

But she slapped me a third time, shouting, "You're an introvert, Stevie! That's what's wrong with you. You're introverted. Your problem is, you're introverted!"

"Shut up," my father said. "I want some peace."

I fell backwards trying to get away from her, struck the end table with my elbow and knocked the Infant of Prague doll onto the floor. It was a possession she valued, having won it at a church raffle. It was one of the consolation prizes, the big prize being a Nash Rambler, which was won by the sister of an alderman who had donated a lot of money to the church the year before. Anyway, the doll broke and its head with the gold crown bounced across the rug. "Now look what you've done!" my mother cried. "The only thing I ever won!"

I didn't care about that doll, which could be purchased for something like $4.98 at any religious artifacts store, but I was stunned by the word "introvert," so stunned that for a minute or so I couldn't speak. I figured I knew what she meant by that word. I remembered something and the memory was too powerful to be anything but meaningful. Once, working as a busboy with her at the Governor Bradford Room, on a Thanksgiving Day when they needed all the extra help they could get, I overheard her say to another waitress, " I sure hope Stevie doesn't grow up to be like those two," referring to two guys who were working there as waiters that day. At the time, I'd thought, "What? Waiters? What's wrong with being a waiter?" And that memory was followed by another. We'd been driving through Boston in a snowstorm and we passed a man walking a dog. "I hope you don't grow up to be like him," she said. "Oh, do you know the guy?" I asked, surprised because it didn't seem likely they could know each other. But she hadn't answered. She was like that. There were some real sticky silences with my mother. But one of the waiters had been what you might call effeminate and the dog had been one of those small, fluffed up dogs, the kind rich old ladies put pink ribbons on and parade around at dog shows, obviously not the kind of dog a real man would keep. In my mother's eyes these men were "introverted" or queer, and now she'd decided that I was, too. After all, I'd never had a steady girl. I'd mostly just hung around with the guys. And I was still a virgin at nineteen and it looked as if I was going to remain one for a while.

Then I knew why she thought I'd been bounced from Sacred Heart, and I started to yell. "I'm not I'm not I'm not I'm not I'm not I'm not—I'M NOT!" I didn't quit until I ran completely out of breath. In the silence that followed, we could hear the Hallorans, who lived downstairs, pounding on their walls. That's what they did when we had a ruckus. They pounded on the walls. Fat lot of good it did them. But they'd gotten in the habit. So they pounded.

My father got up and left the room. We all knew he was going to the kitchen to get a beer. In other words, it looked as if he was starting again. We heard the refrigerator door open with a resigned sigh and then the clink of the beer bottle against the drinking glass. Then, coming through loud and clear, we heard Bishop Sheen's voice. He was saying, "Chastity. Chastity. Chastity."

Brian laughed. "I guess the spokes of his wheel aren't supposed to bring us as close as I thought they were."

"Will you quit making fun of him," my mother said, looking up from where she was kneeling by the broken doll. "He's a bishop."

"Yeah," Brian said. "He's a big wheel."

The phone was ringing in the alcove off the hall. I figured it was Ralph calling and I rushed out to answer it. "Hey, Valyo," he said. "What's going on over there?" He could hear my mother yelling at Brian.

"We're having a fight. What do you think?"

"Ah, you Irish."

"Don't you Italians fight, too?"

"Yeah, but not like you Irish."

"No, you use tommy guns like Al Capone. What's up, Ralph?"

"I talked to the foreman the way I said I would and he told me to bring you around tomorrow. There's an opening if you want it. Meet me at the bus stop at seven-thirty and I'll take you down there."

"Jeez, Ralph, what can I say?"

"You don't owe me nothing. It's just something you do for a friend."

*

After I hung up the phone, I didn't go back into the parlor, but went right to the room I shared with Brian, got into my pajamas and crawled into the upper deck of the bunk bed we'd been sharing since I was ten years old. I was tired, having had to get up at five o'clock that morning to catch the six o'clock bus out of Manchester, not to mention running around all day job hunting, but it wasn't just a matter of being tired. It was because I didn't want to face my mother. She'd say, "Who was that on the phone?" I'd say, "Ralph Ultrino. He got me a job at the paper box factory. He's taking me down there tomorrow." No problem, right? Wrong! After what she'd revealed about her suspicions, "he" had become a loaded word. And Ralph was too good-looking. Everything had changed. My relationship with my mother had become a mine field through which I was going to have to pick my way like a dazed recruit during basic training. From now on, as far as she was concerned, I'd go it alone, with no friends at all, because in her eyes all close friendships were signs of being "introverted." Since that's the way it was, I'd learn to live with it, but it was going to be hard, going it alone that way. It made me want to cry, but then, well… It was wrong to cry, too. So I didn't.

I was just about to drop off to sleep when Brian came in. "We're going to play cards in the kitchen," he said. "Want to play?"

"No."

"C'mon. It's bridge. We need a fourth."

"No, I don't want to."

He leaned on my mattress with his elbows. His face was close to mine. I turned my head away. I buried it in the pillow. "Look, Stevie," he said. " I know it's hard. Who would know better than myself, right? Don't I have to put up with it every day? Don't I have to come home to all this craziness every day after work? But you have to forgive her. She's your mother and she's not well."

I didn't answer.

"Ah, Stevie, don't act like a kid. Grow up."

I took my head out of the pillow. "You heard what she called me."

"She can't help herself. It's the pressure she's under. And it's her body. It's what her body's doing to her now. It's hormones. And, Jesus, Stevie, she's forty-two years old and she works six days a week for minimum wage and tips and she has to put up with that miserable Greek son of bitch. What do you expect from her? She works till she's ready to drop and then comes home to... Home to what? To more tension, more pressure. She's a tough woman, but how much can she take? Say you forgive her. Just say it. She's upset now and she wants to think you're not mad at her."

"I can't say it," I answered.

"C'mon. Stevie. It's such a little thing. Please."

"No."

"O.K. Suit yourself," Brian said. Then he went out, closing the door with a deliberate softness behind him.

Brian would tell her I'd forgiven her anyway. I knew he would. And he'd be right to do it. All I'd done had been to lay myself open to feelings of guilt. I was angry. I had refused to show compassion. I wasn't honoring my parent. I wouldn't forgive even though it was my own mother. I'd have to confess all this on Saturday afternoon, but until I felt truly sorry, what was the point? I couldn't be absolved of my sins until I was sorry I'd committed them and there was no real sorrow in me.

I fell asleep and some time during the night I had a dream. I'd hoped I'd dream about Ralph Ultrino. First I'd told myself it would be nice just to dream about going somewhere with him, doing something, playing ball or swimming. Then I had to admit that a sexy dream would be nice, too. Well, you outgrew all that. But, I'd work at growing up tomorrow. One sexy dream about Ralph wasn't going to hold me back all that much. But my dream wasn't about Ralph. My dream was more profound than the one I'd hoped for. And I surfaced out of that dream like a diver who knows, as he slides like a knife to the bottom of the pool, that he's just experienced the most perfect dive of his life. In my dream, I'd been down on one knee, lacing up my boot. I'd looked up suddenly and seen a naked man standing in front of me. This was no ordinary man. You might almost say this was some kind of spirit. He had a glow to him. He said, "Why be afraid, Stevie? It's all right." That's all there had been to it. I woke up to the sound of the old house cracking and popping in the intense cold and to Brian breathing heavily, deep in dreams of his own, in his bunk down below. As I came up through waves of good feeling, like a diver in a pool, I heard myself say, "Yeah. Right. Good." Because in the dream there had been no contradictions, no problems, no ironies. In the dream everything simply was! But look! It had been a naked man! Well, sure, but that was a phase you went through and some guys, like myself, we took longer to pass out of it than others. See, the thing was, you got laid and then it all cleared up, like acne.

3

"Hey, don't waste any of that. Paper don't grow on trees, y' know."

I was standing in a bin shoveling bits of cardboard into a pulping machine and she passed by on her way to the women's toilets for her five minute break. At Pawtucket Paper Box, where I'd been working for two weeks, they gave you a five minute break every couple of hours. So she'd passed by on her break and made a little joke. Paper don't grow on trees.

On her way back, I said, "Oh, yeah! I get it. 'Paper don't grow on trees.' Ha!"

"Yeah," she answered. "Ha ha!"

The second time I saw her was in the Tip Top Diner, where I went with Ralph every day for lunch. I saw her steal a tip. Or rather, I thought I saw her steal a tip. In that crowded place, with so many people coming and going between the booths, and given my less than 20-20 vision... No, I saw it. I definitely saw it. No mistake. I saw that little hand scoop up that change as she slid into the booth across from ours and I was shocked and angry. As the son of a woman who earned her bread working as a waitress, I knew the one thing you never did—never ever!—was steal a tip. She was with a big guy in a leather jacket, a regular ape, and if I'd been the guy I'd have taken the money out of her hand and slapped it back on the table. But he didn't. Maybe he didn't see her take it. I don't know.

Ralph saw me staring at her and said, "Keep away from that. You can do without that."

"Do you know her?"

"Her name's Luanne. She went with Tom McGrath for a while. You don't need that. You can do better than that."

"Why don't I need it, Ralph?"

"Because she's bad news. O.K., O.K. You want to hear her story? Here's her story. She told this to Tom and he told me. She was married to some guy in Saint Louis, see? One night she stole five hundred bucks from his wallet and went to New York. When she got there, she phoned him and said she was in Chicago and asked would he come and get her."

"Why'd she do that?"

"Because she'd just stolen five hundred bucks from him!"

"So did he go and get her?"

"He went to Chicago, sure. But she was in New York, spending his money and laughing her ass off at him."

"Are they still married?"

"Jeez, I don't know. But would you stay married to her after a stunt like that?"

Later, as we were finishing up, she stopped by our table. I could see that the guy she was with thought she was interested in Ralph. But Ralph just glared at her. It was me she'd stopped to talk to and that made me feel proud. This woman, who was older and had been around, had stopped to talk to me, Little Stevie! All of a sudden I had status.

"You're out of your bin," she said.

"Yeah, they let me out of my cage to eat. My keeper don't deliver," I answered.

"Ha!" she said. Then she left, trailed by her ape. She was a lot shorter than the ape. He dwarfed her. Ralph looked at me and shook his head.

"Why not?" I asked.

"Man, if you don't know, what good would it do for me to tell you?"

The third time I saw her was at the entrance to the subway on a Friday afternoon after work. Usually I left work with Ralph and rode home with him, but he wasn't with me that day. It was the kind of March afternoon when, as you move toward the MTA subway, your eye is caught by something bright, the first bright thing you've seen in months, and as you look up you notice some old woman selling jonquils from a pushcart. But that sensation, that flash of yellow, only lasts for a second, because people are pushing you from behind. As I went down the steps, Luanne was beside me all of a sudden. "A woman selling flowers," she said.

"Yeah, like spring."

"Almost," she said.

"Yeah, it can't be long now. Just a few more weeks."

The subway smelled like the bottom of a diaper pail. It was like every wino in Boston had pissed in there at one time or another. And someone had drawn big hairy cocks sticking out of the pants of all the male figures on the billboards and big tits on the female ones. We pushed through the beat-up old turnstiles. This separated us for a minute, but then we came together again on the platform. The pissy smell was replaced by the smell from the third rail—a chemical smell like mothballs, fractured electricity. I got those smells every day, so usually I didn't notice them. But today my senses were alive to them. I don't know why. It felt good though, feeling alive that way.

"How far do you have to go?" she asked.

"Out to Southie. When I get there, I transfer and catch a bus." "Southie" meant nothing to her, I could see. She wasn't a native.

"I go to Park Street," she said.

"Then you came down the wrong entrance. You need to go up the ramp over there, cross over and take the car going the other way."

"I know how to go. I do this every day."

"What? Come down the wrong entrance?"

"No, go to Park Street. I get off there and catch a car to Charles. I live on Charles Street. It's on the back side of Beacon Hill."

I said, "I know where it is. And you can't get there from here."

She didn't make any move to go over the ramp though. She just stood there. For a minute or two we didn't talk. It wasn't awkward or anything like that. I felt at ease with her. So she stole tips. So she'd lifted five hundred bucks from her husband and run off to New York. What did any of that have to do with me? We were just two people standing on a platform waiting for a train. It was O.K. Finally, though, I said, "I got promoted today. Monday they move me upstairs."

"That's good."

"And it's only the end of my second week."

"That's good. That's very good."

"My name's... My name's Steve," I said.

"My name's Luanne."

"Yeah, I know."

Again, we didn't talk for a while. Then I noticed she was carrying a book. She saw me looking at it. *The Sun Also Rises* by Ernest Hemingway. He'd been in all the papers recently because he'd crashed his plane in Africa.

"You bring books to work?" I asked.

"I read on the subway," she said. "What do you do after you get out to Southie?"

"I eat supper." What else? What a dumb question.

"I mean, after that. Do you ever come back into Boston? I mean, it's Friday night. I'm having some people over. If you're not doing anything, call me. I'm in the book. Under Hanks. L. Hanks."

"I'm probably doing something," I said.

"Well, I..."

My train roared in with a terrific racket, so I couldn't hear the rest of what she had to say. The doors flew open and I stepped forward into a wall of people. "I'll think about it!" I shouted over my shoulder. But by the time I got myself turned around so that I could look back out the windows, the train was rocketing through the tunnel. Something else was moving fast too—Luanne! Well, I thought, she better not wait by the phone, because I wasn't going to call. And yet, she was interested in me. An older woman, interested in me! Maybe this was the answer. Maybe this was my future looking me in the face!

My past was looking me in the face too, though. Some high school kid in an athletic jacket pressed against me as he moved toward the door. His butt was locked against my leg for a minute. Then the car rammed itself around a corner and he fell backwards against me. I grabbed him by the arm to keep him from falling any farther. I could feel his body heat through the jacket. His hair brushed against my face. I could smell the hair oil. He whispered, "Holy shit!" Then he laughed. He was embarrassed. I didn't laugh. When he got off I had to fight the urge to follow him. That might be a kind of future, too. But I didn't want it. It was too scary. My knees felt watery all the rest of the way to my stop. And I had sweat on the palms of my hands. No, you had to fight those impulses. They were immature. It was time to grow up now. It was time to get laid.

No one was home. My father was either at Sullivan's Bar with his cronies or he was driving a cab. He'd gotten a job with Yellow Cab. My mother was at the Governor Bradford Room, working. And Brian was at the Mangan's. I knew this because he

31

had written "Having supper at the Mangan's" at the bottom of the note my mother had left on the kitchen table. It was like the note she left every day before she went to work. It read, "Warm up creamed codfish balls in the fridge. Boil potatoes. Thaw out frozen peas. Put instant rolls in oven at 350 degrees." I decided I wasn't hungry.

Brian was at the Mangan's a lot these days, which was only right, because everyone knew he and Mary were getting married now. He'd told my mother and she hadn't put up any fuss at all. To everyone's surprise, all she said was, "It's about time!" And then, "I want you out from underfoot anyway." There hadn't been any formal announcement yet, no dinner for both families, no banns announced in church, but everyone knew they were getting married, probably in June. They'd started to look for a place to live and they spent a lot of their free time going through furniture stores looking for bargains. Mary had a good job with an insurance company in Copley Square, but neither of them were the type to throw money around foolishly.

So anyway, I had the flat to myself and the silence was eerie. To be in a place where we'd done so much shouting and to hear nothing but the humming of the refrigerator and the ticking of the kitchen clock made me restless, itchy. Nothing to do. Nothing on television except Howdy Doody. No real music to listen to, just a pile of records with fuzzy dust on them, things I couldn't believe anybody had ever wanted to hear—Bing Crosby singing Christmas carols, John McCormack singing Irish ballads, stuff like that. The Infant of Prague doll on the table, its head stuck on with liquid cement. The Maryknoll Missionary Magazine with a smiling nun holding up a Chinese baby. High school yearbooks, Brian's, mine.

I walked around, trying to work off nervous energy. I looked into my parents' bedroom. I saw the double bed they'd shared for twenty-three years, the pink comforter, the two pillows. My mother slept on the left side, my father on the right. In all that time, they'd never changed sides. Twenty-three years like that, back to back, breathing the same air, fighting each other for the warmth of the same cotton blanket. There was nothing in the room but the bed, a bureau, a rag rug and a crucifix on the wall. The crucifix had been coated with a phosphorescent paint so it glowed in the dark. They got married during The Depression. On their wedding day they had five bucks to spend, five big ones. So they took the subway to Boston, which cost a dime, and went to a movie, ninety cents for the two of them. It was *Trader Horn* and was about a jungle princess, a blonde who ruled over a native tribe in the middle of Africa. They never forgot that that was the movie they saw. It was such a big deal. It was their wedding day, after all. When the movie let out, they walked in the Public Garden and rode on a Swan Boat, which cost five cents, but a couple could ride for seven. Later they saw a man standing on a street corner selling strawberries for ten cents a box. My father said, "Eileen, can you make strawberry shortcake?" My mother said, "You bet!" or something like that. So they bought a box and came back to this flat and had shortcake. My grandfather had paid the first six month's rent on this place for them as a wedding gift. Otherwise they couldn't have gotten married at all. Then, after the shortcake, they probably made love.

They were both virgins. I knew this because that's what my father told Brian when they had The Big Talk when Brian was sixteen. I guess my father figured one talk like that was enough to last a lifetime because when I got to be sixteen he didn't say anything to me. Anyway, they made love on their wedding night, or if not on that night then on some other night, because Brian came into existence and then they kept at it and I came into existence. And now Brian was getting married and he and Mary would make love and their kids would come into existence. It just went on and on like that forever and ever, world without end, amen.

I flipped open my yearbook. Here was Vin Romano accepting the Most Cooperative Athlete of the Year Award from Coach Flynn. Ro looked happy and proud accepting the award, with his slick pompadour and his big Mr. B collar. He was a quarterback, a star. The day after graduation, he'd joined the navy. He'd be cooperative in the navy too. He'd probably become an officer. You could call what I'd felt for him hero worship but you couldn't call it love. What happened to all the love? Well, you outgrew it. Ro had outgrown it. Part of outgrowing it had been learning to hate me. That's what growing up was all about.

I found a book, *Studs Lonigan*, on the dresser in our bedroom and started to read it. Brian had brought it home from the drugstore, but my mother knew it was on the list of immoral books mentioned in *The Boston Pilot*, the newspaper they sold from the back of the church after Mass. It told you what movies you couldn't see and what books you couldn't read. Naturally they had a fight over it. My mother said, "You're endangering your immortal soul!" But Brian said, "I'm free, white and twenty-one. I'll read what I want to read. It's my constitutional right as an American citizen!" So she'd given in, which was why the book was still around, but we both knew it could disappear when her mood changed. I really got into that book! It was about an Irish kid growing up in Chicago. It was about us. I'd never read anything like that before. When I looked up, hours had passed and I'd read forty pages. And I hadn't felt sick to my stomach. It was dark outside. The streetlights had come on. There was a change in the sound from the traffic in the street. The tires seemed to be saying, "Get outta the house! Get outta the house! Friday night Friday night Friday night!" It was like a command. To be reading a book Friday night, even if you were enjoying it, meant that something was wrong with you. Nothing wrong with Little Stevie though! So I threw on my peacoat and hit the streets.

*

I went to the Alhambra, which had a double bill, *Knights of the Round Table* and something else. I walked into the lobby during the intermission, right after the "something else" had finished. There were hundreds of people there, milling around, smoking, drinking Cokes, lined up for popcorn, and everyone seemed to be part of a couple except myself. I thought about that bowling date two weeks earlier with Mary's cousin, Theresa. She'd gone back to Providence after her visit and that had been that. She'd been an intense, studious girl, very prim, almost prissy, who could only talk about her classes at Rhode Island University. She was majoring in music and played the flute. I mean, she didn't have any other topic of conversation. But if she'd been in South Boston tonight, I'd have asked her to go to the movies with me. It would be better than being alone. I'd even have enjoyed listening to her talk about her flute. Anything but this!

Then, as I was standing in the candy line, I realized that there was one other person here who was alone, and it was Kevin O'Bannion. So he'd been released from Mass General and here he was, standing in the middle of all these happy, laughing, talking couples, looking lonely and lost. What would drive a person to cut his wrists like that? What kind of misery had driven him to that? What grief? I stepped out of the line and moved toward him. All his clothes looked brand new—the white buck shoes, the flaring pegged pants with the big cuffs, the pink shirt with the red tie, the floppy camel's hair coat. There was something else different, too, but I couldn't quite place it. The eyes were the same though. They had an awful sadness in them, as though he'd opened some door in his head and looked down into a terrible darkness.

"Kevin! How are y'? Good t' see you. What are you up to these days?"

I put out my hand to shake his hand, but he didn't shake mine. I thought, he's still got bandages on his wrists. I didn't see them. I just knew. He said, "I got a job with Mutual Benefit." His eyes seemed to be searching my face. Did he expect me to hit him or something? "Clerk-typist. I do some filing. I'm starting at the bottom, but I intend to move up. I want to be an adjuster some day."

"Yeah, Kevin. You'll make it. You got ambition and you're smart." I was just about to ask him if he wanted to sit with me. But he looked off across my right shoulder. I followed his gaze. A beautiful, well-dressed woman was moving toward us through the crowd.

"Lois," he said. "My fiancee."

And they went off into the theater together. Even Kevin had someone! And the thing that was really different about him was, he'd dyed that streak of white in his hair. Unless you'd known him before, you'd never have guessed it was there. Kevin looked like everyone else now, except for his frightened eyes. And I guessed that he was working on that. He'd get that problem straightened out any day now and then he'd be indistinguishable from any other normal guy.

*

Knights of the Round Table was one of those pictures where you wish the actors would step aside so you could look at the trees. The scenery was terrific, but all those jerks in iron suits kept getting in the way. A few minutes before it was over—that is, just before the lights came up, exposing me as the only person there who wasn't part of a couple—I went into the lobby and looked up a number in the phone directory. It was there all right—Hanks, L., 417 Charles. But should I call her? I decided to flip a coin. It rolled off my palm and bounced across the tiles of the lobby floor. Some guy was standing there having a smoke. He covered it with the toe of his pointy shoe. When he lifted the shoe I saw that it had come up heads. That meant I should call her. The guy looked like some kind of gangster. I decided to leave the quarter there for him.

"Hello, hello, hello," she said, laughing. There was a lot of crashing and banging in the background—party noises, music, voices.

"Hello, Luanne. This is Steve, y' know? From the factory?"

"Hold on, honey. I can't hear you." A door banged shut and then there were no more party noises. "Now. Whoever you are, come on over. Bring a bottle. We're having a blast."

"I'll get there as soon as I can. I'm in South Boston."

"Oh! Oh, you're the guy in the bin! Oh, I know who you are now. Yes, come on over. Steve! Yes! You don't have to bring a bottle. Just bring yourself."

I couldn't have brought liquor anyway. You had to be 21. "I'll be there in an hour," I said. But she'd hung up. The picture had ended and hundreds of people were moving through the lobby. But it was O.K. now. I wasn't alone now. I had a party to go to on a Friday night. I even had a woman, an older woman, who was interested in me. This was fantastic! I belonged! Just to be doing what everyone else was doing, y' know! It felt so good. So good!

*

Charles Street was a fishnet and driftwood neighborhood, the kind of place where people think it's classy to stick a fishnet and a hunk of driftwood in a bay window and call it decoration. There were student rooming houses, bars, bookstores and cafeterias. It was a long way from A Street. Or anyway, it was trying to be. 417 Charles was a four story building with a coffee shop off the areaway in the basement. A note on the mailbox said the buzzer was broken, so don't bother to ring, just come on up. A piece of masking tape had been placed over the latch so that the door couldn't lock shut and a second note read, "Party. 4th Floor. Hanks. BYOB." I went up.

As soon as I got up there and stepped inside, I knew this wasn't for me. I just didn't belong with these people. They were older and they were educated Ivy Leaguers. They went to Harvard or MIT. I could tell. I saw people like this on the subway every day, serious, intense, bearded men with T-squares attached to their belts and pinched, tight girls sitting alone with their knees locked together reading paperback books. The girls always had long hair, arrogant lips and sharp, disdainful eyes. The guys wore scarfs and berets and could probably explain the Theory of Relativity to you in a half a second if you asked them about it. I thought about turning back, walking down the stairs, going home, but, hell, I was here, wasn't I! Besides, it was interesting. There was a whole new world here and I wanted to find out about it. What makes these people tick? What thoughts go through their big egghead brains? How do they see the world? Maybe I could even be a part of all this some day. Just by being here, I was already part of it, right? And so maybe it wasn't all that easy to just turn around, walk down the stairs and go home. Maybe it was already too late for that.

Then Luanne was there, laughing. "Steve, Steve, Steve!" And she took me by the hand, leading me through the crowd, introducing me to people—"Paul and Paulette," "Joe and Joanne." "Phil and Phyllis," "Moe and Mona!" Well, anyway, that's what it sounded like. But what I was really aware of was the pressure of her left hand on my right. It was warm and friendly and reassuring. Again, just as on the subway platform, I felt at ease with her. I thought, "Oh, well, why not!" What she was really doing was showing her friends that I was something special. "Steve works with me in the factory," she told a couple who looked so much alike they might have been twins. "He's the only person down there I really like." And she was doing something else, too—saying to them, "See, I'm not alone tonight. I've got someone." Well, right away, see, we each had somebody on a Friday night, so neither one of us had to feel lonely and left out. The only thing I wondered about was, why me? She could have had some other guy. What did I have to offer someone like her? But always before, on dates in high school, I'd had to take the responsibility for the girl, because that's what the man was supposed to do. I had to pretend to be interested in her. She didn't need to show any interest in me. In fact, she could be haughty or mean or bored, and it was O.K., because she was the woman, and she could be that way if she wanted to be. But I liked Luanne's way much better. She actually seemed to like me. Fantastic!

Still, I had to tell her the truth. "This isn't my kind of thing," I said.

"What is your kind of thing?" she asked. She was being provocative in a kidding kind of way. She gave me a sidelong look that was supposed to be sexy. But she did it in a funny way. Then she laughed.

"I don't know. But not this. I don't go to college. I just work in a factory."

"Well, don't worry. I work there, too. These people are just friends of mine from Boston University. I used to go there before I ran out of money and had to go back to work. I was a psych major. Worked in the psych lab. Ran rats through the mazes. Relax. I won't let them harm you."

What I knew about Boston University was what I read in the papers, mostly the *Record-American,* which my father bought for the race results and the ball scores. Two professors had been kicked out for being Communists. Of course, the *Record American* claimed there were Communists in all the colleges, except for Boston College, of course, which was a Catholic school. If there'd been as many Communists around as the *Record American* claimed, we'd all be Communists and the revolution would've taken place years ago.

"I can handle it," I said.

"I'm sure you can," she answered, handing me a glass of red wine. "Here. Do you like wine?" Wine? Well, what experience had I had? A glass with spaghetti when I ate supper with Italian friends. On an impulse, I drank it down in one gulp, and it went right through my empty stomach into my brain. It was grainy and black and powerful, a fast one-two, pow right to the moon! I fell back against the wall, laughed in a crazy way and said, "Whee!" For a second I didn't think I could hold it down, but then I shuddered once and was O.K. It was so bitter it brought tears to my eyes. I heard her say, "Vino Fino. Dago Red." Then she leaned forward into my fiery breath and brushed away the tear that was rolling down my cheek. Her eyes never left my eyes. Then she walked away and I was talking to some guy whose brainy, big-browed head stuck out of his turtle-neck sweater like a large inquisitive cucumber. Nothing he said made any sense to me, but I kept nodding to him and saying, "Uh, yeah! Yeah, sure. Right! Absolutely!" Albert Camus, you bet! Bertrand Russell? I was reading him yesterday! Plato! Right. Jean-Paul Sartre? We're like brothers, him and me! When Luanne came back, she'd refilled the glass. I didn't want any more, but I took it just to be polite. So then I had to look around for somewhere to put it. There were no tables in the room, just two concrete blocks which she must have lifted from a construction site. Who had carried the blocks up four flights of stairs? One of her boyfriends? That ape in the Tip Top Diner? Anyway, the concrete blocks supported a record player. I finally put the glass on a window still. That was smart, because all of a sudden everyone was dancing, including Luanne and myself. The song was "Cherry Pink and Apple Blossom White." It was a mambo. Look Ma, I'm doin' the mambo! Me, Little Stevie!

"You're good," she said. "A good dancer. You feel the rhythm in your whole body, in all your muscles and bones. Most men don't."

"Yeah, I'm good," I said, laughing to cover up the embarrassment I felt. I didn't want her to think I was any different from most men. Luckily it was dark in the room and she couldn't tell that I was blushing right to the roots of my hair. "I mean, I feel good. I feel very good."

"That's why they grew the grapes," she said.

*

But the good feeling didn't last. For five minutes or so I was witty, funny, on top of the world, dancing around like Fred Astaire, but then a wave of anxiety swept over me that made me break out in a sweat and go weak in the knees. At first it was vague, just a general feeling of uneasiness, but then it localized and I knew I had to call home. It was midnight and no one knew where I was. They'd be combing the neighborhood for me. My mother would be having a nervous breakdown. "I have to call home, Luanne," I said, separating myself from her. "Where's your phone?"

"In the bedroom," she said, motioning toward a closed door at the other end of the room. "Hey, are you O.K.?"

"Oh, sure. Yeah, I'm O.K. I'm fine."

I pushed open the door. There were no lights on in there. Two guys were standing by the window. Their heads were close together, their bodies were close together. They moved apart when I came in. It all happened in a split second in a dark room. "I have to use the phone," I said. "I need to make a call." I said this in a real breathy way, almost a whisper. It was because I was surprised. They were just shadows against the window glass. But then I felt my body respond. I couldn't control it. I wanted to close the door behind me and stay in the dark room with them. I think one of them had been holding the other around the waist. I wanted to hold a guy around the waist like that. Then another feeling passed over me and I was angry at them. They had no right. Not in someone else's apartment. Not at a party like this. Not at Luanne's. And then I felt scared to be in a room with these two guys. I didn't even know who they were. And they were queer. "Look, it's like... Like an emergency," I said, finally. "I have to call."

They went out and closed the door behind them. I had been too embarrassed to really look at them. I sat on the bed, which was just a mattress on a box spring, and dialed our number.

There was no answer.

That didn't make sense. There was always someone home after midnight. Both my mother and Brian worked on Saturday, so they never stayed out late on Friday night. I hung up and dialed again. Again there was no answer.

Luanne came in. "Is anything the matter?"

She handed me a glass of something. I sipped it and it tasted like cherry-flavored cough syrup. I put it down on the floor. "What is it?"

"Sloe gin. I thought you'd like it better than the wine."

I was sitting on the bed. She was standing in front of me. I put my arm around her waist and buried my face in the large skirt she was wearing. I felt the body heat, the warmth, the comfort of it, the tenderness. After a few seconds of this, I stood up and we went back into the other room where we danced again, a slow dance this time, a song called "Teach Me Tonight." I liked the smell of her hair. I liked the way she hummed the song in my ear. It felt good not to be alone. Did you say I had a lot to learn? Yeah! Well, don't think I'm trying not to learn. Uh-huh. Since this is the perfect spot to learn. Right! Teach me tonight. You bet.

But naturally I kept trying to phone. When I finally got someone, it was my father. I told him I was at a party and not to worry about me. "Well, you enjoy yourself, son," he said. "You're only young once." I knew he thought the party was in our neighborhood and I decided to let him go on thinking that. It was just too difficult to explain what I was doing on Charles Street. I wouldn't even have known where to begin.

"Is everything all right at home?" I asked.

"Well, yes. Yes. Your mother and myself, we were over at the Mangan's for a while, but we're back now, sitting here at the kitchen table, havin' a beer and talking. You have fun, Stevie. You work hard all week and you deserve it." He meant it, too. Good old Jack Riley, everybody's friend. He knew how important it was to have a good time. "We'll leave the back door unlocked for you. We'll see you in the morning."

"Is Brian home yet?" All of a sudden I needed to talk to my brother. There was something I had to ask him.

"No, he's still out with Mary. We'll see you tomorrow, Stevie. You take care." And he hung up.

There was an alarm clock with an illuminated dial sitting on the floor next to the bed. It was 12:50 A.M. The subways had shut down at midnight, so how was I going to get home? I could call a cab, but I didn't have enough money for the fare. I could ask Luanne to loan me some money and pay her back at the factory on Monday, but did a man ever ask a woman for money like that? And what if she didn't have it? That would be so embarrassing. Well, I could get a cab, ride out to Southie and ask the driver to wait while I went upstairs to get the money from my father. But if the party had been in our neighborhood, why had I needed to take a cab home? And what if my father was asleep when I arrived? I'd have to wake him up. O.K. then, I could walk home, through the Public Garden and the South End, even though it would take an hour or more and the streets were dangerous.

But Luanne solved the problem for me. She came into the room, sat down beside me, took my hand, kissed it once and then said, "Why don't you stay here tonight?" I could smell perfume. Had she just put it on fresh? It was kind of nice. I liked it.

*

The party broke up in a brawl, just like parties in South Boston. These people weren't so different after all. Just before the fight, everybody went off into separate groups, some into the bedroom, some into the kitchenette, some into the hall. A woman who'd had too much to drink got the idea her husband was locked in the bathroom making out with her best friend. He wasn't. He was in there alone. When he stepped out, though, she hit him anyway. He yelled, "Hey, what is this!" He pushed his wife and she fell down. Immediately, everyone was there, yelling, taking sides, arguing, pushing, complaining. Then they all cleared out, grabbing their coats and stampeding down the stairs, leaving me alone in the middle of the room with Luanne, staring at ashtrays, beer cans, wine bottles and half-filled glasses. The party was over.

"I don't know why I do it," she said. "It's always like this. I don't care anything for them and they don't care anything for me. It's the same every time I give a party."

"They never stay to clean up?"

She threw her head back and laughed. Her teeth flashed. "Oh, Steve," she said. Then she turned and went into the bedroom.

I didn't much want to follow her in there. I waited a few minutes and then went to the doorway. She was sitting on the bed looking up at me.

"Why me?" I asked. It wasn't the way it was supposed to be. The guy was supposed to pick the girl. The guy was supposed to make all the moves. It hadn't happened that way. From the very beginning, it hadn't happened that way. And it wasn't happening that way now. "I mean, why did you pick me?"

Her voice sounded tired. "I like red-headed men. They're different."

"Yeah," I said sarcastically. "We're a different breed."

"You don't like being different?"

41

I didn't answer. I just stood there. Whole minutes seemed to go by.

"Well, and it's your voice," she said. "I like your voice. I lived with a guy in New York who had a voice like yours. I'm attracted to your voice. Why don't you come over and sit down beside me?"

I did. This was going to be O.K. We were going to make this O.K. I started to relax. Still, I wasn't able to make myself look into her face. I just sat there staring down at my hands folded in my lap. "What was this guy like?" I asked. She placed her hand gently on my leg.

"Oh, a complete madman. Owned three books, all by Dostoyevski. He hit me once with *Notes from Underground*, the only thin book Dostoyevski ever wrote, thank God. If he'd hit me with *The Brothers Karamazov*, he'd have killed me. Anyway, he loved those three books more than anything in the world."

"Sounds like a pseudo-intellectual."

"He was a writer. Juiced out of his head most of the time. He used to lock me in the apartment when he went out. Afraid I'd run out on him. I was all he had, except for those books. He went out one day and came back with the words 'Cry for Lonely' tattooed on his arm. He said he did it so he'd always have some way to remember me. His name was Barney Kerrigan."

"Oh, he was Irish."

"Yes, a crazy Irish writer with blue eyes that could bore right through you. Anyway, he had a voice like yours."

"I'm more than just a voice."

"Oh, I know. I know. It's not only your voice. There's a mutual need. You need me. I need you. It's reciprocal. We could be good for each other. I like you. I can see that you like me. So we have that."

"Yes," I answered. "I guess that's it."

*

We were lying naked side by side on our backs. I started shaking all over. "What's the matter?" she asked. "Are you cold?"

"Yeah. Cold"

She got up, naked except for her bra, and went to the closet. I watched her ass. I had never watched a woman's bare ass before. It was different from a man's. She came back with a big puffy comforter and put it over me. Then she eased in beside me. Her body was warm against mine. But my teeth kept right on chattering. "The alcohol lowered your body temperature," she

42

said. "That's why you feel cold." But except for the glass of wine I'd slugged down, what alcohol had I had? One sip of sloe gin, that's all.

"Look," I said, finally. "I have to tell you this. I don't know anything. You're going to have to teach me everything. I never had the experience before. I mean, I never had intercourse before and... It's just that no woman has ever wanted me before and, well..."

She didn't answer right away. She was thinking it over. Then she said, "You have to want the woman first."

"You'll have to tell me what you want," I said.

"I want you," she answered. And I believed her. Absolutely.

*

I kissed her on the eyelids, the cheeks and then the lips. Part of me was watching me do this from some distance away. But I was very tender. I could kiss very tenderly. It was all right.

I said. "Guys always say a woman only wants what she can't have. Is that true?"

"Perhaps. But a woman always gets what she wants, if she's smart. You're very nice. You're very loving."

"Do women like men to be loving?"

"Sometimes. You're still trembling."

"I'm still cold. Can I ask you something? It's personal. Don't get mad. But you've... You've had a lot of men, right? Why? I mean, why so many?" It was a stupid thing to ask but I asked it. I didn't even really care how many men she'd had. But the question was out.

"For love," she answered. "Always for love. Here, let me help you. Give me your hand. That's my heart beating. Feel it? You've never touched a woman's breast before, have you? Don't be afraid. You don't need to be afraid. Trust me. I'll show you how." She was smiling. Even in the darkness, I could see that. It was a nice smile. It was reassuring. She knew what to do. I just had to let her lead me. It would be O.K.

*

She had stopped smiling. "What's wrong? What is it?" she asked.

"Impossible."

"Why do you say that? What's impossible?"

I withdrew from her and threw myself on my back. I looked up at the ceiling. I had an erection. That wasn't it. Something else

43

was wrong. I'd been in her. I'd slid right in. That was no problem. It was something else.

"What are you thinking?" she asked.

I didn't answer. I could have answered, but I didn't. I held it in.

"Are you thinking you're abnormal now because you didn't have an orgasm with me."

"Maybe."

"Nonsense. That's nonsense. Why, you're not out on the streets picking up little boys!"

I rolled away from her.

"Listen to me, please," she said. "You drank alcohol. The alcohol's inhibiting you. That's all it is. It happens all the time. It's normal. It's nothing. In the morning you'll be able to do it."

"I didn't know this would happen. If I'd known, I'd have told you and we wouldn't have gone through this."

"Don't be silly. How can you ever know ahead of time?"

"I knew."

"That's not possible. You can't know how your body's going to perform. Even men who've done it thousands of times can't know. Please don't take this to heart. It happens all the time. Are you listening to me?"

"Yes."

"Don't worry. Believe me, I understand. I understand completely."

"Do you?"

"Yes, I do, damn it. This is nothing! And if you weren't so inexperienced, you'd know that."

"I want to go to sleep now."

"No, not that way. Not with that tone of voice."

"I want to go to sleep."

"Not till you listen."

"Let me go to sleep."

"Not till I convince you."

"Look, I don't care how many guys failed with you. A hundred, a thousand, I don't care. All I care about is... I failed with you!"

"You're so selfish. You can't even see what this is doing to me!"

"Aw, you'll live!"

"I was out of my mind to get involved with someone as young as you."

44

"I'm almost twenty. How old are you?"

"Twenty-six. God, you're only nineteen and a virgin, too. Why, I never go to bed with virgins. There are too many experienced men around." She laughed as if she'd just remembered some private joke. "And I always said I wouldn't be one of those bitches who ruins children."

"I'm not a child."

"What? Oh, God, you're so funny. O.K., sweetie, I won't call you a child. I mean, I'll stop calling you a child when you stop acting like a child! And you can start calling me a woman the day you finally grow up. Honey, I've got a child, a four year old child! He's in New York with his father. And, believe me, at the age of four he acts more like an adult than you do. Where have you been all your life, under a rock? Nobody's a virgin at nineteen! Nobody! You are a selfish, spoiled little boy!"

She was doing this to get me angry. It was deliberate. I could see that. It worked, too. I was angry. So what else could I do except respond? I climbed on top of her, gripped her by the wrists and entered her again. No problem there. I could pound away too, mechanically, like a piston, trying to make my mind a blank as I did it. This is what I was supposed to be doing. This was expected of me. This is how a real man responded. She closed her eyes and began to respond, also. It crossed my mind that she was faking it. But no, it was O.K. This is what she wanted. It was starting to be O.K. for her. No problem on her part. The problem was mine. Something in my mind kept me from coming. Something in my mind kept me from feeling. Something in my mind kept me from caring. Something in my mind kept me from wanting this. She began to make noises, as if she might come, and at that moment I thought again, "She's faking it!" But I pounded away, because I was a man, performing the way a man should perform. I was indifferent to being inside her. It didn't mean anything to me really. I was just there. It made it official. The big change could take place now. I was finally a man. I could go up on the stage now so Coach Flynn could give me my letter in fucking! Oh, wow. At that moment a feeling of aversion swept over me. It was involuntary and it only lasted for a second, but it was enough. I withdrew. I hadn't come. I didn't want to come. I was finished. It was over.

But she seemed to have arrived. Yes, she hadn't faked it. Or had she? What difference did it make? None! Maybe she had only pretended because she wanted me to come. She opened her eyes. I could see the question forming there. She didn't ask it. She

45

didn't need to. The answer was no. I hadn't come. Neither one of us spoke. The expression on her face changed. A long time passed. Then she sighed, punched at her pillow a couple of times, raised the comforter to her shoulders, rolled over and went to sleep.

4

I woke up. I couldn't see Luanne, buried the way she was under the comforter, so I gathered up my clothes and went into the other room. Before I got dressed, I looked down at my body. It was a tight, trim body—chest, belly, cock, balls, tough little legs, a runner's body. Yeah! In nineteen years it had never let me down. It hadn't let me down last night either. As long as I could keep my mind a blank, it had performed the way it was supposed to perform. But how was it supposed to perform? Smoothly, efficiently, mechanically, like a car with fluid drive? Like a new Buick Road-master? Sure, but there was one problem. I wasn't a car. Now where had I left my glasses? All of a sudden I just wanted to get out of there, go home, take a bath, get into my own bed, go to sleep there under my own blanket with my head on my own pillow. But I also felt it would be wrong to walk out on Luanne at six in the morning without a word. But hell! She was experienced. She could take it. Probably lots of guys had walked out on her in the past in just this way. That made me feel bad. How terrible to wake up in a place like this, knowing the guy hadn't even thought enough of you to hang around to say goodbye. And nothing to do on Saturday morning except clean up the mess left by the phony friends who'd run out on you the night before, friends who also hadn't bothered to say goodbye, friends who were waking up now next to wives and husbands and lovers they could kiss awake, talk to under the warm blankets, eat ham and eggs with later, walk on the Common with in the afternoon, feed bread to the ducks in the pond. How terrible to wake up alone on a Saturday morning with no one to spend the rest of the day with. At least I could leave a note. But what could I say? "Call me?" At my parents' house? "Thanks. I had a good time." Forget it!

I went back into the bedroom to wake her up. A cold blue-gray light was falling through the uncurtained window and a cold blue-gray pigeon was parading back and forth on the window ledge on the other side of the glass. I could hear it cooing numbly and mindlessly to itself out there. Beyond the ledge and the pigeon was the whole cold blue-gray city of Boston. There were a million people out there. They were all just about to wake up into conscious life. I stood there looking down at the shape under the comforter and I knew I couldn't wake Luanne up. What would I say to her? We'd said everything that needed to be said last night as far as I was concerned. And what if she drew me down beside her and said, "Let's give it another try?" There weren't going to be any more tries.

I left.

*

The subways were running again and I was back in South Boston before seven o'clock. As I crossed Broadway I noticed that they had painted a fresh green stripe down the center of the street for the Saint Patrick's Day parade next week. My father would march in a green suit with the Sons of Erin, as he had every Saint Patrick's Day since I could remember, carrying his shillelagh, that knobbed stick, symbol of potency, of authority, of Ireland itself. I'd stand on the curb with my brother and, possibly, my mother, to watch him go by. As a kid, I'd felt proud. Wow! There goes my father in a parade! Now I knew it was all bullshit, but I'd stand there and wave at him anyway, just because I knew it made him feel good to see me there. The bars would be selling beer at ten cents a glass and you wouldn't need to show an I.D. to get a drink. They'd serve anyone on Saint Patrick's Day. I'd never been drunk before, but maybe it was time for me to tie one on. After all, everyone got drunk on Saint Patrick's Day. It was the thing to do. It meant you belonged. You fit in. You were part of the group. After the parade, there would be a party at our house for relatives and friends, and then a big shindig at the Sons of Erin Lodge Hall which would go on till everybody dropped at two, three, four in the morning, because Saint Patrick's Day was the big event of the year, the affirmation of our national identity, our culture, our collective life. Our collective life was going to work every day for minimum wage, worrying about being laid off, voting the straight Democratic ticket and getting drunk to numb the pain. But once a year we were Captain Lightfoot, fighting the British. We were Saint Patrick,

48

driving out the snakes. We were the Blarney Stone. We were Barry Fitzgerald. What more did we want?

Then I was home, at the old three decker, and what a relief that was! I crept up the outside stairs and let myself in the back door. It had been left unlocked, just as my father had said it would be when he talked to me on the phone. I was sure everyone would be in bed, but I was wrong. My father was sitting at the kitchen table, drinking coffee and reading the *Record-American*. I saw his bent back, his shoulders, his bald spot. I'd seen him like that hundreds of time, but this morning it was different. Then he turned around, saw me and said, "Ah, my other prodigal son! I was beginning to think we'd lost both of you."

It didn't make sense and my first thought was that he'd been drinking, but no, he was sober. He had, in fact, had his drinking pretty much under control since his last trip to the hospital. "Well, no," I answered. "You didn't lose me. I just stayed out all night, that's all."

"I never took you for a tomcat, Stevie."

I looked at him, thinking he might be proud of me for being a tomcat, but he wasn't proud. He was just tired, too tired to care one way or the other, tired of the work, tired of the booze problem, tired of family problems, tired of my mother's change of life. Yeah, a man got worn down by it. But how old was my father? Forty-six, forty-seven? Well, he'd started work at fourteen and it had been heavy labor. Who wouldn't get worn down? And while I was looking into his face, that big pug Irish face with the purple veins broken out around his nose, I almost broke down. I mean, I almost wept. He's my father, I thought, and I love him, and, yes, he's on his way down, and he can probably count the number of years he's got left, but... I didn't cry, naturally. If I had, he'd have had a heart attack right there and then. It would have finished him off right then. But I felt like crying, and it felt good to know I could feel something, even if it wasn't convenient to express it right then.

"Stevie," he said. "Your brother ran off with the Mangan girl yesterday. They drove down to Connecticut in her car and got married by a justice of the peace at seven o'clock last night. He called about nine o'clock to tell us. They're still down there, honeymoonin'."

"Brian?"

"Do you have any other brothers?"

"Brian? Brian ran off and got married?"

"Your mother thinks he got the girl pregnant. Why else would they run off and get married that way? She's so upset, she's not going in to work today. She took a pill and went to bed. Be nice to her today, Stevie. She's all broken up about this."

"Brian got Mary pregnant?"

"Now we don't know that, son. That's just what your mother thinks. The Mangans are upset, too, naturally. We were over there last night and Ethel said she had been looking forward to a big wedding because Mary's her only girl. She kept saying, 'Why couldn't they wait! Why couldn't they wait!'"

"'Wait?' They been going together for seven years!"

"Sure, but if they waited seven years, why couldn't they wait three months longer? What was the big rush? This is a painful thing, Stevie. Your mother's so ashamed. She thinks the whole neighborhood's talkin' about this. Some day, when you're a parent yourself, you'll understand though. You bring up your kid right and you expect him to do the right thing and then he pulls a stunt like this. It gets to you. It really does. I thought your brother had more self control."

Like Brian should have kept it in his pants! I wanted a bath. I wanted a bath in the worst way. I wanted to wash everything away. I wanted to start the whole game over again. I wanted to play by a whole new set of rules. These rules my people played by were evidence of insanity. I was living in a lunatic asylum and I wanted out! Now! My father ran on and on, talking about Brian as a baby, cute things he'd said and done, how fast kids grow up, the trouble they get into, how kids didn't listen to advice from their parents nowadays. And I fidgeted and squirmed. Finally I couldn't stand it any more. I said, "I just got to take a bath!" and I ran into the bathroom and filled the old claw-footed tub. After I got in and immersed myself, it occurred to me that no one rushes home at sunrise and jumps immediately into the bathtub after being out all night unless he's been with a woman, and probably not a very nice woman either. I figured I had no secrets from my father now on that score.

When I came out, wrapped up in an old bathrobe, he'd cooked breakfast for me—fried eggs, bacon, toast. He'd even squeezed oranges for juice. And since I hadn't had solid food since noon the day before, I fell on it like a starving wolf. After I'd eaten, I realized he couldn't look me in the eye. In the process of proving myself a man, I'd become a disappointment to him. That was it, wasn't it?

"You will be especially nice to your mother today, won't you, Stevie? I'd be much obliged to you if you'd do that. Don't give her anything additional, if you know what I mean." That was his main concern now, to shield her from any additional stress. Their marriage worked that way sometimes. When there was a crisis, he shielded her. And she shielded him sometimes, too. When there wasn't a crisis, they were more or less indifferent to each other, but lately there'd always been some kind of crisis, so they were close now. "Can you do that, Stevie? As a favor to your father?"

"Yes," I said.

"I want you to give me your word on it."

"I give you my word on it," I said.

*

Studs Lonigan was lying on the dresser where I'd put it the night before. I crawled up into my bunk, got under the blanket and opened it. I read about Leon. I'd read this part last night, but not the way I was reading it now. Leon "middle aged and fat, with a meaty rump that always made the guys laugh, and a pair of breastworks like a woman, skin smooth and oily, eyes dark and cowy, lips thick and sensuous. 'I say! Why do boys look backward? I always wanted to know,' he said in a half-lisp. Leon placed his hand on Stud's shoulder, and patted his head with the other hand. It made Studs feel a little queer. He felt as if Leon's hands were dirty, or his stomach was going to turn, or something like that."

I closed the book. Then I closed my eyes. Until last night, there'd been a way out. There'd been a door. Everyone told me the door was there. Open the door and pass on through. The door was sexual intercourse with a woman. After you opened it and passed on through, you weren't queer. For me there'd never been any door. They'd told me there was a door and maybe there was—for them! But not for me. For me it had been an illusion. I had opened nothing and passed on through nothing and I was where I'd always been. I was back at the beginning. I was queer. But I wasn't anything like this Leon guy. My lips were thin, my stomach was flat, my skin was clear and I had never lisped, not even as a baby. But there must be queers like Leon around, though I couldn't remember ever having seen any. And if there were, I'd have to spend the rest of my life with them. What kind of job could I get? How would I support myself? How would I survive? My whole body felt frozen all of a sudden, as if I'd died and been placed in one of those refrigerated compartments in the police morgue. No amount of intercourse would ever make me anything but what

51

I was. I loved men. I'd always loved men. That's all I'd ever wanted—just to love men. I was queer.

*

It took me a long time to fall asleep and when I woke up, about one in the afternoon, I felt as if I wanted to stay asleep forever. I had no desire to come back into the waking world. I opened my eyes on anxiety, a crackling anxiety in my body, in my mind, and I'd never experienced anything like this before. The intensity of that anxiety was so fierce! I could hardly force myself to get out of bed. I just wanted to stay there forever away from everyone else in the world.

But I got up and went into the kitchen. My mother was there, eating a chicken salad sandwich. She looked up. I could see from the marks under her eyes that she'd been crying. It was because of Brian. But before I had time to feel sorry for her, she snapped at me. "Where were you last night!" No preliminaries with her. No social amenities. Just right out with it. O.K., let's fight! I'm ready. But then I remembered. I'd promised my father.

"I was at a party."

"Where?"

"In Boston. Where's Dad?"

"Driving his cab. I thought you had more sense."

I sat down at the table, facing her. She was sitting where my father had been sitting earlier. I'd given him my word. But there was no way! I decided to wade right in. To hell with my word! "What? What 'sense?' You're the one who isn't making sense. What are you talking about anyway?"

"You were with a woman, weren't you?"

"So what? That's what I'm supposed to do. I'm a man."

"Oh, you're so smart! You've always been such a wise guy! But you know what I'm talking about!"

"No, I don't. Honest to God, I don't. You were worried because I wasn't dating. So you had Brian fix me up with Mary's cousin and I had to listen to her talk about her stupid flute all night. You thought there was something wrong with me because I didn't have a girl. Now you're mad because you think I was with a woman. What do you want from me anyway?"

"You aren't stupid! You can guess what I want."

"No, I can't. Maybe I am stupid. Maybe you're going to have to spell it out for me. But tell me. Please tell me. What do you want from me?"

52

"I want you to go to confession and get the sin off your soul."

"What sin?"

"You know what sin."

"I don't. There are so many of them. I lost track. Which one?" Then I could see that she was about to cry and I felt so sorry for her. She didn't deserve all the things that were happening to her. I said, "O.K., O.K. I'll go. I'll go to confession. I was going to go anyway. I'll go at five o'clock. I'll be there at the church as soon as the door opens. I want to go! I need to go!"

"Ah, then you were with a woman?"

"Isn't that what you already decided?"

"Then you admit it?"

"You knew the minute I was born I'd go with a woman some day!"

"Yes, but not this way. I thought better of you."

"No, you didn't. You thought worse of me. Much worse!"

So it was out in the open now and I was ready to argue with her about it. But you couldn't win in any argument with my mother because she had the ultimate defense and it was territorial. "Get out of my kitchen. Get out of my house. Get out of my sight. Don't come back in here until you've seen the priest and done penance. Just get out of here. Out—now!"

"Where am I supposed to go? I live here!"

My peacoat was resting on the back of a chair. She picked it up and threw it at me. I caught it. "Go to church, Mister High and Mighty. That's where you can go. To church! And don't come back in here until your sins have been forgiven!"

*

A dozen old women in kerchiefs and padded jackets and floppy overshoes were lined up at five o'clock at the door of the church. They looked like Russian peasants. To make it even more perfect, it had started to snow. All we needed were some howling wolves chasing a sled. It was Lent and people are more conscious of sin during the grim, iron-gray days of Lent. So here they were, lined up waiting for the doors to open so they could file in, kneel in the confessional box and void their sins on Father Dolan. None of them spoke to me, but they knew I was there all right. Their eyes slid sideways when I joined them and they saw me and they knew. Only a really important sin could bring a young man like myself to the church door on a day like this at this hour. And of course they knew what my sin was because there's only one important sin. I had had sex. I hadn't a clue as to what their's could be. Maybe they thought about sex as they sat home rocking and fingering their rosary beads and the thought was enough. Yes, that must be it. These women were sick, in physical pain, probably a little crazy. They'd suffered through the pains of childbirth and menopause. Their husbands had beaten them, cheated on them and finally abandoned them in death. I recognized one of them as old Mrs. Hurley, who used to run a candy store. I said, "Hello." I tried to smile. You do what you can to make it better.

Father Dolan unlocked the door at seven minutes past five—seven minutes that felt like seven thousand years in Purgatory because the wind, which was blowing directly from the north, was as raw as an Irish potato. We went inside. The building itself was a damp, dimly lit barn designed by somebody who wanted the parishioners to feel even worse about human existence than they did ordinarily. Life was continual torment. We were passing through a Vale of Tears. There were Seven Mysteries and they were all Sorrowful. You can't escape the cross. Life was a continual ache in the crotch. You offered up the pain to God.

I slid into a pew, knelt down and began to examine my conscience. I'd been doing this every Saturday afternoon since I was six years old, and it should have been automatic, like putting a car into neutral and letting it slide smoothly forward. But it wasn't automatic. No. Not this time. There was only one sin, what I'd done the night before. That was it, one sin. It had been seven days since my last confession and surely I'd done something else, something that was an offense in the eyes of God. But no, there was nothing else. I hadn't missed Mass, eaten meat on Friday, lied or stolen anything. I almost wished I had, because it would make my confession easier. My single sin was going to stand out like one lone, bold word on a billboard. So the only sin was sex. Well, so what else was new? Sex is the only sin. You got that from the age of six. The nuns drilled it into you. They knew all about it, of course, never having had anything to do with it in their entire lives. Was being sarcastic about nuns a sin? Sure! It showed disrespect for lawful authority. Yes, but you had to take pleasure in the sarcasm.

"Oh my God I am heartily sorry for having offended Thee." But how had I offended Him? I'd offended Luanne. She'd said, "I want you." and I hadn't delivered. Or had I? Well, if she had an orgasm, I guess I delivered. But she may have been faking it. Sex without orgasm was a sin too, right? Maybe not. Well, faking it was a sin. That was a lie and lying was definitely a sin. Well, but that was Luanne's sin, not mine. I hadn't faked anything. Well, I hadn't told her I was queer. But I didn't know I was queer. How could I not know? I knew. Yes, but I knew in a different way. Well, now I knew definitely, right? Right. But how did I know? I knew it in my body, in my cock, in my balls, in my ass, in my tongue. My nipples knew it and the tips of my fingers knew it and my muscles knew it. I knew it in the palm of my right hand and in my autonomic nervous system and in the pupils of my eyes. My cerebral cortex knew it and my medula oblongata knew it too. Every cell in my body had been whispering it to me for years and I'd pretended not to listen. But it was coming through loud and clear now. I was queer.

My turn came so I left the pew, lifted the stiff curtain, stepped into the confessional and knelt down in the icy darkness. When Father Dolan finished with the person on the other side, that gate slid shut and my gate slid open. I could see the shadow shape of Father Dolan in there. I heard him say, "You may begin." I tried to begin. But nothing came out. He tried to help me, "How many weeks since your last confession?"

"One."

"Go ahead."

I couldn't speak. My tongue was numb.

"'And I detest all my sins.'"

"And I detest." Silence.

"Just tell me your sins. That will be enough."

"I only committed one sin," I said.

"And what was that sin?" he asked.

"Intercourse!"

Well, I'd blurted it out. I'd done it. I should have felt relieved. But I experienced no feeling of relief. Why not? Because I'd sounded proud of it. That's how it had come out, loud and proud. Well, a guy was supposed to be proud of it. I had intercourse with a woman. That made me a man. Well, O.K. That was the right response when you were hanging out in front of the drugstore with the guys. But in here you were supposed to feel sorry for it. Well, I was sorry for it. I'd have given anything if I could just go back in time and undo what I'd done. It was true sorrow, too. It was honest remorse. But all that was secular. It had nothing to do with Father Dolan, the Catholic Church or God. It was just a personal thing. And I hadn't enjoyed it. I'd heard a priest say once, "Sex is a necessary evil and no sin if you take no pleasure in it." And at the time I'd thought, "Well, but there's always pleasure in it, so it's always a sin." Well, I'd been mistaken about that, apparently. But not taking pleasure in it was wrong, too. It meant I was queer.

"Son, there are many people waiting to confess."

"I'm sorry, Father. I didn't enjoy it. Is it a sin if you don't enjoy it?" He shifted around in there. Maybe he hadn't heard me. I had, in fact, whispered it into the wooden shelf where I was resting my elbows. Then a kind of bitterness took hold of me. It came out of nowhere and gripped me all of a sudden. I heard myself say, "Is it only right to do it when you don't want to do it? Is it only right when it's like a religious duty that you hate to perform and you do it because you want a kid and there's no other way to get one?" He was hearing this. I was saying this loud and clear.

"I think you know the answers to the questions you're asking me. Have you been drinking?"

"No, I haven't been drinking. And I don't know the answers to the questions I've been asking. I'm asking you about sexual intercourse. I had intercourse with a woman and I didn't enjoy it. Does that mean I didn't sin?"

He wasn't in the mood for this. He'd probably had a long, hard day, and he was certainly feeling the pressure from all those women waiting in the pews. He also had a time schedule. He had to be out of here by a quarter to seven. I was a bastard to bug him this way. It couldn't have been much fun for him sitting in a box in this cold, moldy church, listening to people like me talk about sin.

"Your attitude is all wrong," he said, sharply. "I want you to leave the confessional now, go to the altar and pray for a change of heart. You're putting your soul in jeopardy with your belligerent attitude. It's dangerous. Remember, you are communicating through me directly to God the Father! You're being disrespectful to God the Father!"

"But you're a priest! You're supposed to give me answers!"

The gate banged shut and I was cut off. As far as I knew, I was the only person who'd ever been denied absolution this way. Ordinarily I'd have been afraid. But I was beyond all that. "Wait! I have another sin," I said. "I just remembered."

The gate slid open again. "Go ahead," he said.

"I'm reading an immoral book."

"What's it called?"

"Studs Lonigan."

"Stop reading the book."

"Why!"

"Why? Did you ask why! Are you questioning my authority? Are you kneeling here in this confessional and questioning my authority? Did I hear you ask why! You can't read the book because the Church has decided that the book is dangerous for you to read. You put your soul in jeopardy when you read it. That should be enough for you."

"It's not enough," I said.

That did it! He said, "Young man, I am ordering you now to leave this confessional, go to the altar and pray for a change of heart. You have placed your immortal soul in great danger by defying the authority of my office. I am a priest. This is the confessional. I am attempting to administer a sacrament. Do you understand where you are? Do you understand what I'm telling you? Are you capable of rational thought at this moment? Do you understand what I'm saying?"

For several seconds I'd been aware of someone standing on the other side of the curtain, waiting to take my place in the confessional. Whoever it was had heard the gate bang shut and come forward, thinking I was finished in there. I looked around the edge of the curtain and saw a little girl in a snowsuit. She was seven or eight years old, no more than that, and she had her hands folded in that First Communion way the nuns teach you. Her eyes were closed and her lips were moving. Suddenly, though, her eyes popped open and we were staring at each other, our faces less than a foot apart. She was startled and for a second I was afraid she was going to cry out.

"Do you understand me!" Father Dolan said again.

"No!" I answered.

The gate banged shut again. I thought he might come out, collar me and drag me out of the box. As far as I knew, no priest had ever done that in the whole two-thousand year history of the Church. But there was always a first time.

As I stepped out of the box, allowing the girl to scurry in, I found myself looking down into the upturned face of Sylvie Donovan, who was kneeling in a pew there. Sylvie lived in a house three doors up from ours and was my mother's friend. They had coffee together a couple of times a week at the doughnut place a few blocks from the drugstore where Brian worked. Sylvie had heard everything we'd said in the confessional. I could see that in the shocked expression on her pale, frightened face.

5

Brian came home on Sunday afternoon. My mother was working, but my father was there. They talked for an hour in the kitchen with the door closed. When Brian finally came into the bedroom, where I was reading *Studs Lonigan,* he was smiling. He looked great—radiant, glowing! I got charged up just being in the same room with him.

"I dropped Mary off at her parents' place. But she's going to meet me at church at three o'clock for Benediction," he said. "Want to go to church with us?"

I didn't want to go to church but I did want to be with Brian. I'd been sitting around all day wishing he'd come home so that I could talk to him about what happened Friday night. If I could get it off my chest, maybe I could get rid of this dead feeling in my body. If talking to Brian didn't help, I was in trouble, because who else could I go to?

"You bet!" I said, grabbing my coat.

It was still snowing, and as he drove through the stark white streets in my father's old Studebaker, Brian kept shifting down because of the slickness. I should have let him concentrate on his driving but the need to talk was powerful. "Brian, why'd you do it?" I asked.

He laughed. He was in a terrifically good mood. "Oh, we both decided we didn't want the fuss of a big wedding. After all, who's getting married, us or our parents? This is what we wanted, so this is what we did. I mean, we made the decision and we did it."

"Ma thinks Mary's pregnant."

"I know. I just talked to Dad about it. Well, Mary's not pregnant. Ma's wrong. All the couples she's known who've run off to a j.p. to get married have done it because the woman was in trouble. But Mary and myself, we're the exception to the rule. Ma's got everything figured out ahead of time, so she can't deal with the exceptions. She's always been that way."

I was looking at Brian's hand on the steering wheel. He had a ring on his finger now. Married! Brian was married. It changed everything. He was wearing a new overcoat, a new hat, a new tie, a new shirt. Everything was new. Under all the new clothes, though, he had the same body, the same permanent heart murmur, the same susceptibility to viruses. Last night the body had been naked in a bed in a motel room in Connecticut. Last night he'd made it with his wife. He'd make it with this same wife for the next forty or fifty years. It was hard to imagine. He'd do it thousands of times to my one time. And it would always be with the same woman! I guess you'd really have to like her. "How was the honeymoon?" I asked.

He laughed. "When you get married," he said, "don't spend your honeymoon in Putnam, Connecticut. It's not all that exotic when you come right down to it. But otherwise, yeah, it was great."

"It must feel great to have made up your mind to do something and then to have gone ahead and done it."

"Yeah, it feels great. I recommend it."

The windshield wipers were flashing and flipping away at the snowflakes. Ka-flip, ka-flip! I looked out at the streets as they swept by—three deckers, warehouses, schools, a police station, a church, a cemetery. I'd seen it all before and it never changed, and because it never changed, it was safe. My father had been born a block from here. His father owned that building and lived in it for forty years. Our great-grandfather, the one who came from Ireland, settled down ten blocks from here. Our people made one trip, the big one across the Atlantic, and that was enough for them for the rest of all time. Because what more did they need? A street, a house, a bed, a table, a wife, a kid. "Sometimes I think I'll never be happy unless I get out of here," I said.

"Do it. Live your life. What else is there?"

"But how? How, Brian? That's what I'm asking myself now. How?"

"Put one foot in front of the other. Then put the other foot in front of that one."

"That's all there is to it?"

"That's all there is to it."

"Yeah, Brian, but look! So Mary's not pregnant, but Ma thinks she is! So you're going to have to convince Ma she's not. You and Mary don't have a place to live yet, so you'll have to live with us. And Mary will have to live with her parents. Isn't that going to cause problems? And what about money? Mary's not pregnant now, but some day she will be, and you'll have to support a wife and kid. Mary has a job now but won't she have to quit that when the baby comes? How are you going to do all this on sixty-five cents an hour from Rexall Drug?" This is what came from living your own life. Then I remembered that I'd started to live mine on Friday night and I said, "Brian, can I ask you a question about something? It's important."

"Sure. Shoot."

But we'd come to the church and he had to pull into the parking lot. The lot had been cleared for the morning Masses, but that had been hours ago, and it had been snowing steadily since. The back wheels spun around and the car skidded sideways. This wasn't the right moment to talk. Then, after we finally got the car parked, we saw Mary standing at the door of the church, so there was just no way. My relationship with my brother had become nothing but a series of questions I never seemed to get the opportunity to ask.

*

Monday was bright and sunny. All of a sudden it was spring again. The snow melted away and I saw a crocus in someone's yard. At work, they put me on a cutting machine, under a big sign that read BE CAREFUL! THE MISTAKE YOU MAKE TODAY COULD RUIN THE REST OF YOUR LIFE! About eleven o'clock I looked up and saw Luanne standing there, staring at me. I was startled and almost lost a finger to the machine. Then she went away without saying a word. But I couldn't think about her. I had to concentrate on what I was doing. The foreman came by and said I was doing fine, so I felt good. But it was hard, clearing everything out of my mind and placing that machine in the forefront. It was hard, but it was good, too. I didn't want to think about Luanne and there was my machine right there in front of me insisting that I think about it instead. I hummed away to myself, happy to have this task to perform.

At noon, with the rhythm of the machine still circulating through my body, I went over to the Tip Top looking for Ralph. I'd missed him at the bus stop earlier and had to come to work alone. So I was looking forward to eating lunch with him. I wanted to lose myself in that feeling of friendship we could generate between ourselves sometimes. That was very important to me, being able to laugh and joke with Ralph in the diner. But when I got there and could see around the crowd, I noticed that he was sitting in a booth with Luanne, and I knew, from the expressions on their faces when they saw me, that they'd been talking about me. If you'd hit me over the head with a hammer I couldn't have been more stunned. Oh no! My face went white. They could see how shocked I was. On Ralph's face I read contempt. Contempt for me, his friend! On Luanne's face, I could see what looked like concern, but I wasn't buying it. Everything anybody'd ever told me about not trusting a woman came back to me. Guys you could trust! But women? Forget it! As I slid into the booth across from them, she reached out and touched the back of my hand. I shook it off. "Honey," she said. "We have to talk!" Hadn't she already talked enough?

Ralph got up, saying, "I guess I'm not hungry after all. I'll see you all later."

"Hey, Ralph! You don't have to go. Stay!"

"No. You need to talk to your woman. I'll meet you on the loading platform later. See me during my break."

I was looking up. Ralph was looming over me. There was nothing else to look at except Ralph, his coveralls, his thighs pressing against the legs of his coveralls, his cock and balls pressing against the crotch of his coveralls, his chest pressing against his workshirt, which was open at the neck so that some curly black hair could tumble out. Then I knew that Ralph knew. Italians always knew. They just didn't talk about it. Or they kidded you along. Ralph knew how I felt. Ralph had always known. I looked up at his face. He was angry. He kept staring down at me. I couldn't outstare Ralph. I lowered my eyes.

Right at that moment, the waitress came over. "The Special today is chicken croquettes."

Luanne said, "Chicken croquettes? Tried them once. Didn't like them. Never tried them again."

"Maybe you should give them another try," the waitress said. But she was looking at Ralph, not Luanne. "I'd give it another try. Really. They're good today."

"O.K. I'll give them another try," Luanne said.

"I'll go with you now, Ralph," I said.

"No, you stay here. Listen to your woman. She has something to tell you. Listen to her and listen to her good."

"I don't want to listen to her!" I said. And when I looked up, Ralph was gone.

"I thought you might have done something to hurt yourself," Luanne said. "I wanted to call you, but there are fifty Rileys in the phone book and half of them live in South Boston. Why did you walk out on me that way, Steve? Why?"

"I'm sorry it happened, Luanne."

"Don't say that."

"It won't happen again."

I looked across the table at her. I had been inside her body. It had meant nothing at all. If I went back in there a thousand times, it would still mean nothing at all. All Ralph had to do was knock against me with his arm or his shoulder or his leg and I was electrified instantly into life. All Ralph had to do was stand there! It happened automatically. It was too fast for conscious control. If she knocked against me, it would mean nothing at all. It was as simple as that.

"I don't want to hear any more of that," she said. "We'll make it again sometime. Or if you don't make it with me, you'll make it with some other chick. You didn't even know me and it was your first time. That was it. I should have let you know me as a person first. It just happened too fast."

"It would have been the same if I'd known you a hundred years. It's just the way I am."

"Look, I know men in New York who are... who are that way. You're not anything like them. What do you know about it anyhow? Tell me."

"'Ballet is the fairy's baseball,'" I said.

"What's that mean?"

"I read it in the *Record-American*. It means queers dress up, put on mascara and go to the ballet in New York."

"Have you ever been to a ballet?"

"No."

"Do you even know where you can get tickets for a ballet?"

"I guess you just go to the theater. The box office."

"What else do you know?"

"During a full moon we go crazy. We have 'periods' the way women do, except it's in our minds. We get incredibly horny. We can't control our impulses. We become sex crazed. The jails fill up. They round us up and throw us in jail. It's the only way the police can control us. I read it in *Washington Confidential* while I was killing time in a drugstore on Saturday."

62

"Steve, this is ridiculous. You're as masculine as any man I ever met. I was the wrong woman for you, but don't turn away from all women because of me. Besides, you were fine. You satisfied me. There are worse things for a man than not ejaculating."

"What?"

"Well, ejaculating too soon. Then they can't satisfy the woman."

"Did I satisfy you?"

"Of course. You stayed erect the whole time. There's nothing wrong with you. You're fine. You're going to have lots of girls and you're going to be happy."

They had these wall jukeboxes in every booth. Over the noise of the crowd, I could hear The Chordettes singing "Mister Sandman." *Send me a dream. Make his complexion like peaches and cream.* "I know how you feel, Luanne. But what can I do? You made a mistake when you picked me. You'll get over it." *Give him two lips. Like roses in clover.* "But you shouldn't have talked to Ralph. You had no right." *And tell me all my lonesome nights are over.* "He's my friend. If I want to talk to Ralph about my sex life, that's fine. But not you. You shouldn't have done it." *Give him a loving heart like Pagliacci. And lots of wavy hair like Liberace.* "I'm sorry about Friday night. I'm sorry I left without saying goodbye. But you had no right to talk to Ralph."

"All I said to your friend Ralph was that you walked out on me. Ralph's a very conventional young man. Walking out that way violates his code. That's all. Look, Steve, I know where you're at. I don't know how many times I thought I must be a lesbian because I felt close to a girlfriend. But it doesn't mean a thing."

"If it doesn't mean a thing, it must be different for women. Because it sure means something to men." I stared off toward the counter. I saw a wall of newspapers there. People were sitting there reading them. The headlines read McCARTHY McCARTHY McCARTHY! He'd been looking for Communists under the bed. He didn't find any there, so now he was looking for queers *in* the bed. He was obsessed. The whole country was obsessed. Everyone was trying to ferret out queers. I'd even heard one guy telling another guy that he thought McCarthy himself was queer! *Mister Sandman. Send me a dream. Make him the cutest that I've ever seen!* Queers were everywhere. But they were also nowhere. You couldn't tell when you'd finally found one. They were so sly. They blended right in. They lied to you. They hid. Well, there was one sitting right over here in this booth. Me! But I couldn't convince the woman sitting across from me.

"Can we remain friends?" Luanne asked.

"Sure, that'll be great," I said. "I have the feeling I'm going to need all the friends I can get!"

*

I was sitting with Ralph at the end of the loading platform. It was over. Our friendship was over. I knew that. This was just the goodbye part. I'd relied on Ralph too long for emotional satisfaction. You outgrew these things. You moved on. This was the last time we'd ever sit side by side in the sunshine out here like this. I kept glancing sideways at the sunshine on his face. Ralph was just too good-looking. Well, I was saying goodbye to that. I was too mature now for high school crushes. He sure did look good there though, my old friend Ralph, with the sunshine on his dark curly hair.

"You don't walk out on a woman like that ever, ever. Even if she is a whore," Ralph said.

"Oh, I don't think she's a whore. She doesn't take money for it. Have you ever been with a whore, Ralph?"

"No. Never."

I believed him. "Do you know where a whorehouse is?"

"Sure. You want me to take you there? It's in East Boston. Look, I'm from a big Italian family. I have twelve uncles. So you think I don't know where the whorehouse is! But I'm going with a nice girl and we're going to get married. What do I need with whores?"

"Most guys make a big thing out of going with whores. Why is that, Ralph?"

He turned his head and looked directly at me. The expression on his face seemed to say, "Why ask me? You're the guy who just went with one!" But what he said was, "Ah, going with a whore, that's nothing. It don't make you a man. What makes you a man is caring about a woman, being there for her, trying to understand her needs. It's a feeling a man has for a woman. You feel it in your heart. Don't listen to the hoods. They're afraid of the women they talk about all the time. Inside, they're scared. I feel sorry for them."

A foreman looked out around the door. Ralph's break was almost over. So was mine. "This is it for me," Ralph said. "I'm kissing this job goodbye. I gave my notice."

"You're quitting?"

"Right. My cousin Nunzio's opening a nightclub in Revere and he asked me to help him manage it. I asked Marie to marry me. We haven't set a date, but maybe in July. We already looked at a house in one of them new subdivisions in Lynn. My cousin Frank said he'd help with the financing. Hey, don't stay in this factory too long. It'll chew you up and spit out the pieces."

Ralph walked away. Ralph sure knew how to carry himself. He had a real sexy walk. There was so much magic in his body, from the heft of his shoulders to the tilt of his hips to the crack of his ass.

I never saw Ralph again.

6

This is my nightmare vision of The Fifties—a city street, appliance stores, show windows filled with hundreds of television sets, every set turned on in the middle of the bright blue sunstruck afternoon, every screen projecting the image of Joe McCarthy— the heavy face, the aquiline sharpness of the nose, the feral incisors, the prominent jaw, the bulging forehead, the receding hairline. Irish taverns on side streets in Boston with their doors open to the spring breeze, television sets over every bar, Joe McCarthy on every screen, his brawny arms pumping, sleeves rolled up for a fight. Beyond the city, suburbs exploding out from the center like the concentric rings of a hydrogen bomb, a television set on in every carpeted living room, with Joe McCarthy holding forth, hectoring, scowling, snarling, snapping, hissing. "Point of order! Point of order!" He was against intelligence, brain power, human thought, civilization, education, class. He was opposed to weirdos, pinkos, crazies, deviants, perverts. He was every schoolyard bully who had ever pushed me down, called me a sissy and kicked me in the ribs. He was Irish. He was one of us. My people loved him. "Don't say nothin' against Joe. He's fightin' the good fight. He's on our side!" Whose side? Not mine! His message was unequivocal: "If you're different, I'll destroy you!"

Some time that spring my mother gave up patrolling the books we read. She had to admit defeat. The paperback revolution was upon us. Every week hundreds of new titles blossomed on the racks in the drugstore where Brian worked. The *Boston Pilot* and Father Dolan and my mother were powerless against this. I bought my first book for twenty-five cents—George Orwell's *1984*. Now, reading it again thirty-five years later (it is 1:40 P.M., May 9, 1989) I try to imagine how I responded, as a nineteen year old gay boy brought up in that environment to lines like, "The Party was trying to kill the sex instinct, or, if it could not be killed, then to distort it and dirty it." "The only recognized purpose of marriage was to beget children for the service of the Party." "The aim of the Party was not merely to prevent men and women from forming loyalties which it might not be able to control. Its real, undeclared purpose was to remove all pleasure from the sexual act." And, "The smallest thing could give you away. A nervous tic, an unconscious look of anxiety, a habit of muttering to yourself—anything that carried with it the suggestion of abnormality, of having something to hide."

I can't remember my responses to specific lines, of course, but I do remember the following exchange with my brother. Brian said, "Hey, I heard about that book. It's about the world of the future."

I shook my head sadly. "No," I said. "It's here. It's now. It's us."

One night, while he was driving his cab, my father was robbed at gunpoint by a Negro. Though he gave him the money, the thief hit him on the back of the head anyway and the cut required half a dozen stitches. My father marched in the Saint Patrick's Day parade that year with a bandage on his head, looking, as Brian pointed out, "Like the Spirit of '76!" People in the crowd cheered my father. But as my father said at the party later, "I'm no hero. Show me a hero and I'll eat me a Guinea sandwich!" He'd given the thief the money because he'd been told on the day he was hired, "You may be robbed. If it happens, give the guy the money. A dead cab driver is no use to us." But a lot of people felt that if his boss hadn't given him these instructions, "Good old Jack Riley would have put up a helluva fight!" The thief was picked up by the police a few hours after the robbery and my father went down to the station house, where he identified him. He was a young guy in his twenties, on drugs.

The first negro I saw after the robbery—it was a guy walking with his daughter, a girl about five years old, at City Point Beach—made me think, "The whole race tried to kill my father!" I felt a flash of rage go through me. "They" had hit my father. "They" had almost killed him! The gun might have gone off. My training in racial hatred was too strong, I told myself. I'd been brought up wrong. I should have been tolerant. But I couldn't be. It was like something in my blood. I was ashamed of myself, but it was there. I couldn't deny it. I hated negroes. Where was that hatred lodged? In my brain? In my body? Who had put it there? And what could I do to get rid of it?

And yet, something good came out of those six stitches. At the party, a friend of my father's, Paddy Milligan, said, "Jack, you're too good a man to risk your life night after night drivin' that cab. Why don't you come to work with me at Sunny Orange. There are routes opening up all over the place now. I can get you one in North Quincy if you want it. All of a sudden every housewife in Boston wants orange juice delivered to her door every morning, and there's no reason why you can't do it."

Almost before the words were out of Paddy's mouth, my father said, "By God, I'll do it!" They shook hands on it. And my father's life was changed.

During that party, also, my mother's brother Tim took Brian into our bedroom to have a talk with him. "You come, too," Tim said to me. "I've got a few things to say to you, too." So I went in and sat in the upper bunk while they talked, sitting side by side down below. I had my copy of *1984* with me. I read a little bit, stopped, listened, and then read a bit more.

"How's your health?" Tim asked Brian.

"It's O.K. I have to watch myself. No heavy lifting. But I'm all right."

"How's it feel to be a married man now?"

"It feels good."

"When are you going to get your own place?"

"We're looking at places. We don't want to rent just any old hole in the wall. Mary's pretty particular."

"What's your draft status now?"

"4-F. Because of my heart. Deferred."

"But you'd go if you could, right?"

"They won't call me up until we get into World War III. But, yeah, I'd go if everyone else went, I guess."

"A man should be willing to defend his country, Brian."

"Oh, yeah. Sure. Of course. That's right, Tim."

I'd heard Tim say more than once, "There are four things a man has to do in his lifetime—fight in a war, fall in love, get married and father a son." Tim had done all of these things except father a son. He'd had a daughter, but no son. Before the daughter was born, he'd said, "I'll get my son into West Point." But it was a girl, so all he'd been able to do was get her into a good dancing school—she was only four—with the daughters of bankers, lawyers and real estate men. As for fighting in a war, Tim had not only done that, he'd been wounded, too, by a piece of shrapnel in the leg. It was only a small shard, "about the size of a lima bean," as he acknowledged, but it was genuine shrapnel. So he had an authentic wound and it was money in the bank. In 1945, a Colonel Cummington had "done something for the brave lad" by taking him on in a management position in his manufacturing plant in Boston, and now, nine years later, Tim had all the things a smart young man on the way up was supposed to have—a ranch-type house with a breezeway and a two-car garage and a patio in the suburbs, a cocker spaniel, a new Pontiac Chieftain, an attractive wife and that daughter in dancing school.

I heard Tim say, "Brian, I want you to think about this. Think hard, think seriously. Consider all the pros and cons, all the angles. Then let me know what you've decided. Business is good now and we're expanding. This summer I'd like to take you on at the plant. You'll start on the floor, learning the business from the ground up. No one down there will know you're my nephew. That will be our secret, yours, mine, Colonel Cummington's. In a year or so, you'll move right on up to a management position, just below mine. We're in a boom time, Brian, and, as I've pointed out to you before, our product, the Cummington fire extinguisher, is the best on the market. And we're about to move into the aerosol can market. The sky's the limit, Brian, believe me."

"It sounds good," Brian responded. "But I'd like to talk to Mary about it first."

"Of course. One of the proudest moments of a man's life is when he's thought a thing through and come to a clear-cut decision. So don't be hasty. What we're talking about here is the rest of your life, so think it through."

"Yeah, haste makes waste," Brian said.

So their little talk ended. Just before Brian left the room, he shot me a look which Tim couldn't see. It summed up everything Brian felt about Tim. When Brian was fifteen years old, Tim had taken him into the den of the ranch-type house after Christmas dinner and read him something from the *Wall Street Journal.* "Copper copper copper!" Tim had said. "Invest in copper." Brian had taken thirteen cents from his pocket—it was all the money he had to his name—and thrown it down on a table. "There!" he shouted. "That's my total investment in copper!" Then he'd walked out. He walked out now. But he hadn't shouted. He had to talk to Mary. Tim had just handed him a future. Brian had someone else involved now. Brian had a wife.

"Now you," Tim said. And I climbed down and sat beside him. He glanced at the book. The glance said, "Reading books, that will get you nowhere!" But he didn't say it. He swallowed it. He had important things to do here, settling his nephews' futures for the sake of his sister. My mother had put him up to this. I knew it. All of a sudden I just knew it. She had talked to him and he was doing it for her.

"You're more fortunate than your brother," Tim said. "You have normal health."

"Yeah, normal health. Normal."

He didn't like the way I said that. So he repeated himself. "Your health is normal, correct?"

"I'm normal," I answered.

I looked at his crew cut, his gold-rimmed glasses, the tight, tanned skin over his cheekbones. He'd been on vacation in the West Indies in February, while the rest of us were up to our asses in snow. But then, as a man who'd made it, he had a right to go to the West Indies if he wanted to. I mean, that's why God made those islands. So people like my uncle could go down there and sit in the sand under a palm tree and soak up the sun. In the other room, I could hear my father laughing with his friends. My father called Tim "Phony Baloney," but not to his face. And never in front of my mother. Tim was my mother's favorite brother and this had been true since they were kids. She had two other brothers who didn't mean that much to her, but, as the only girl in a family with three boys, she had attached herself to Tim and the attachment had lasted. They looked alike. They even thought alike. A stranger would guess they were brother and sister right away, after looking at them and listening to them talk. For my father, though, there was one thing worse than Tim's phoniness and that was the fact that he voted Republican now. "Party loyalty, the straight Democratic ticket," my father said. It was his creed. "You may not always like it, but it's what makes The System work!" He hadn't liked voting for Adlai Stevenson, but he'd done it. And Tim had not only voted for Eisenhower, he'd bragged about it! And yet... Tim shouldered his responsibilities. Tim was trying to help his sister. Tim was being a good uncle. Tim was doing the best he knew how.

"You know you're going to be drafted any day now, Stevie."

"I know."

"You'll go in as a buck private. How do you feel about that?"

70

"Other guys have survived it."

"That's true. But it's a waste. It's a waste of time. You'll never meet anybody there that will do you any good. Just a lot of losers. Stevie, I phoned a friend of mine, Captain Knox, at the Boston Army Base the other day and we talked about you and your future. You know, you could go to OTC and come out a second lieutenant. I can fix it up for you through Captain Knox. You'll have to take some tests, but you're smart. You'll pass them. What do you think?"

"I don't know," I said.

"Ah, how's life at the factory?" He was very good with the sarcasm. It was very subtle, but it was there. You couldn't miss it. It was like my mother only she never bothered to be subtle.

"It's O.K. I'm doing O.K. I like it down there."

"This tough guy pose doesn't fit you, Stevie. What kind of people are you meeting in the factory?"

"Workers," I answered. "People who work. Working men and women."

A long silence followed. We were definitely not at ease with each other. Then he broke the silence by saying, "I want you to visualize yourself in ten years if you stay in that factory. How do you see yourself at the age of thirty if you're still doing factory work at that age?"

At first I drew a blank. Then I saw myself minus a few fingers and toes. Then I saw his point. You moved up into the middle class, you kept your fingers and toes. But I said, "I'll be all right. I'll make out."

"No, you won't," he said firmly. "Now listen to me and listen good!" This was Tim the manager talking. This was the Tim that got those fire extinguishers to those schools and hospitals on schedule. You had to give him credit. He was good at this. "What I'm going to tell you is important. It's based on my own personal experience and experience is the best teacher. You are a young man with no future, Stevie. You have no skills. You aren't enrolled in a college. You went to the seminary and they washed you out. Now wait! Don't interrupt. If you had a commission, you'd learn a real skill, how to motivate and manage other men. Once you learn how to do that, you'll understand how this country runs. The country runs on military principles. The military is our largest industry. Once you're in as an officer, there's no limit to how far you can go. I went in in 1940. Worked my way up. I only have a

71

high school diploma, but that's enough if you apply good management techniques. And they'll teach you those techniques."

"I don't want to be an officer," I said.

For a second I thought Tim was going to get up and leave. A red flush passed along his jawline. It was a very masculine jawline. I imagined that women found him attractive. He was attractive without being sexy, like some movie actors, Lee Bowman, guys like that. He was angry. But he controlled his anger and said, "Look, Stevie, here's the 'given.' Here's what we have to work with. You're going to be drafted into the army anyway as a buck private. You'll be cleaning latrines and peeling potatoes and crawling in the mud. Other men will be telling you to do these things. You'll resent the hell out of them. It will do you no good. You'll be a buck private and that's what buck privates are for—to be pushed around and yelled at and made to crawl in the mud. Stevie, I can get you in as an officer. Then you can be the one who directs the other men! You'll have dignity, self respect and pride. Men will look up to you. Personally, from watching you, I don't think you have a lot of pride to lose. Go in as a private, come out as a private, hit the streets again and you're right back where you are now— nowhere!"

"The difference is, it's a lifetime thing, being an officer. It's a career!"

"Do you have something else planned for your life?"

In the other room, I could hear my father singing "Did Your Mother Come From Ireland?" What did I have planned? Drive a cab? Sunny Orange? My father was no help. Tim knew I had no plans. He had the knife in and he just had to twist it. The bastard.

"Do you see some big golden paper box in your future? Is that it?"

Tim was right. I was doomed. To hell with Tim! "Look," I said. "I get up every day. I go to work. I never miss a day. I bring home a paycheck. I give it to my mother. What do you want from me? I'm doin' the best I can! And I am proud of what I do! A lot of guys don't work. They just hang out. I'm not on the corner drinking Smoky Pete. I work! I'm proud of the fact that I work!"

He nodded. He conceded. I had won a point or two there. He tried another approach. "I talked to your mother, Stevie. She's worried sick about you. She sees what's happening. You're drifting. She sees that. She's a mother who wants the best for her sons. That's natural in a mother. And she sees you going downhill.

72

Stevie, she cried. I held her and she cried in my arms. She said, 'Help him, please! Do something for him. I can't do it!' She wants you to survive, Stevie. She's your mother and she loves you and you're breaking her heart. Now think about it a minute."

I thought about it and then said, "I haven't done anything to break her heart. I'm doing the right thing. I'm working and paying board. I'm doing O.K."

"It's not enough. You should be meeting people who can help you get ahead. What kind of people are you associating with in that factory? Your mother said you've gotten in with a bad crowd there. Is that true?"

Ah, so that was it! "No," I said. "My mother's wrong. I'm not in with any bad crowd. And, no, I don't want to be an officer. Thanks, but no thanks." Luanne wasn't a crowd. And what was "bad" anyway? Maybe having sexual intercourse. Well, but... that's what they told me I was supposed to do! "And it sounds good, yelling at soldiers who are crawling in the mud rather than crawling in the mud myself. But I don't want to do it. I'd probably tell them to get up out of the mud and go take a shower. I'd be terrible at it. I don't want to tell people what to do!"

"Then I'll tell you what to do," Tim said, as though everything up to this point had been just some kind of game. "Your mother's tears really got to me. So I made an appointment for you with Captain Knox on my own. Be at the Army Base next Tuesday at ten o'clock for your interview with him. Don't miss that appointment. I put myself on the line for you with this. This is a special favor that Captain Knox is doing for me as a friend. Do not miss it! Do you understand?"

"Tuesday at ten? What about my job?"

"Forget about the job. We're getting you out of that, too. Your mother will talk to you about that after we finish in here." He stood up. This meant a lot to him—saving his sister's kids. You managed men, you managed your sister's kids. It was a big responsibility. But he was a big man. He had management skills. He was a success. Part of me hated him. But part of me knew he was right. My mother had cried in his arms. Oh, wow. "You'll do all right, Stevie," he said, and his tone of voice seemed to indicate that he was doing his best to convince himself of this. "You're immature, but you'll grow up fast in the army, just like I did. I wasn't going to tell you this, but your mother said, 'If Stevie messes up with this one, he's on his own. I don't want him living in this house anymore.'"

73

"What's she want me to do, pitch a tent in the park?"

"I got the impression she thinks the park will be too good for you. It's cruel, but that's life. You're of age now and it's time you were out on your own. Give your mother a break. She just wants you settled in something safe and secure. She's tired of worrying about you. It's killing her."

"O.K. I'll go see this Knox guy."

"Captain Knox. And remember to call him 'sir.' And do you know how to stand when you face him in his office?"

"No. Show me."

Tim showed me. He braced. I braced. Shoulders back, stomach in, heels together. Tim had a powerful body, big shoulders and chest, but there was no magic in it. It was boring. It crossed my mind that he probably had a lousy sex life. "Remember that everything depends on the first impression, Stevie. Make him feel that you regard OTC as the most important thing in your life. Appear eager and willing." Then he added sadly, "Even if you're not. You're starting with very little so... give it everything you've got." He was looking around at our room, at the beat-up old dresser, the cheap bunk beds purchased from an army surplus store ten years earlier. He was probably thinking, "Well, I'll get them out of this." Or he may have been thinking, "This crap would fetch about five dollars and thirty-seven cents at the Salvation Army junk shop." It sure wasn't his house in the suburbs, though it was certainly where he came from. His father, my maternal grandfather, had come to Boston in the Twenties from a ruined poultry farm in New Hampshire, with four kids and a wife to support, looking for work in the shipyards, which were hiring then. Tim had sold doughnuts from door to door, doughnuts my grandmother had dished up each morning from a big pot of grease on their kitchen range. He had peddled papers, hustled salve, worked as a furniture mover... Life had only one lesson to teach Tim—work, survive and keep your eyes open for the main chance. And he was handing me mine. He didn't know the half of it though. Maybe the army was the right place for me, because, see, in the army I wouldn't have to get married! In business I'd need that photograph of the wife and kiddies on my desk in my office, but in the army.... There must be plenty of guys in the army who did fine without a wife! Yeah. So thanks, Tim! Thanks a lot.

When I came out of the bedroom, I saw my mother standing in the hall. She was wearing the green nylon blouse she wore every Saint Patrick's Day and she had a plastic shamrock in her graying hair. "Do you want a beer?" she asked. And when I nodded, she went into the kitchen and got one for me. People were beginning to leave, to go on to other parties and the festivities at the lodge hall. We stood there, mother and son, saying goodbye to them. I was still carrying my copy of *1984*. She took it and opened it. She read two sentences out loud. "'The sexual act, successfully performed, was rebellion. Desire was thought crime.'"

"The book's not on The List," I said. "It's anti-Communist."

She shrugged. "You're an adult. You can read what you want." She meant it. I was so surprised, I almost dropped my beer bottle. "By the way, Stevie, there's an opening at the Ritz-Carlton for a busboy. I want you to go over there tomorrow and talk to Frank DiPietro, the maitre d'. I've known Frank for years. He used to work at the Beaconsfield. You're qualified for the job. You've worked as a busboy on holidays at the Governor Bradford Room with me. I bought a new shirt and tie for you to wear when you go. And shine your shoes."

So that was it. "But what about my job at the factory?" I asked.

"Forget it. You don't even need to give notice. Just tell them you're through and pick up your check. The job at the Ritz will see you through till you go in the army." Then she added, "I'm not going to ask you to stop seeing the woman you're involved with in Boston. You're of age. You can do what you want to do. But I'll just assume you have sense enough to take precautions, if you know what I mean. You're going into OTC. The last thing in the world you want right now is to knock up some woman. That would really mess up things for you."

"I'll be careful," I said.

She caught the sarcastic tone but didn't understand it. "Don't be smart, Stevie. It happens! You think it can't happen to you, but it can happen. And it can ruin your life. I worry about you."

"Please don't worry," I said. "Believe me, it won't happen. There isn't one chance in a million that it will happen."

"You miscalculate the odds," she said, with a quick, nervous smile.

"No, I don't," I answered, firmly. "Believe me, I don't."

Brian was talking to Mary in the kitchen. You could feel the tension! I stood in the doorway and listened to them. Mary said, "You're the one who has to decide! I can't decide for you."

"But I'd be under Tim's thumb for the rest of my life."

"Whose thumb are you under now?"

"You mean Mr. Trueblood's thumb?" Trueblood managed the drugstore.

"You're going to be under someone's thumb anyway, honey. We all are. I'm under Mrs. Knight's thumb in the office. If you've got to be under someone's thumb, why not get paid well for it? But I don't want to influence you, dear. You decide. And we could get a house. We can't keep living apart this way. It's not a marriage."

"But, Mary, I can't stand the guy! He's a phony son of a bitch. And you met his wife once. You said you hated her. You said all she ever talks about are her carpets and floor lamps. You'd have to associate with her. You said you didn't want a ranch house!"

"But I want some kind of house! I can't live with my mother and father for the rest of my life! I want a home."

"You make me feel ashamed because I can't provide you with a home."

It was embarrassing to stand there listening to them—two married people having a fight and one of them my brother, Brian. Well, this was what came of an act of rebellion. One night in Putnam, Connecticut and a lifetime of this. I walked away. Fighting with a wife like this, it was something I was never going to have to worry about. After all, I was queer.

7

Now I had a procedure which I followed five days a week. First I put polish on my busboy shoes. Then I ironed the gray flannel trousers I was required to wear. Finally, I shook out the stiffly starched white shirt and placed my clip-on bow tie in the pocket, so that I wouldn't forget it. When I arrived at the Ritz, I would be issued a white duck jacket to wear over my white shirt. Then I would be ready to fill the water glasses of Al Capp, Shirley Booth, Senator Wilton Platt of Nebraska, Bishop Houlihan, the Spanish Duke of Castalba, Archibald MacLeish, William Frawley, Vito Antonio Gasparelli and W. Averell Harriman all of whom ate at the Ritz Carlton dining room during the time I worked there. I shared the ironing board in our kitchen every morning now with my mother and since we were engaged in the same occupation— the feeding and watering of wealthy, influential human animals— we were friends now.

She was especially pleased that I'd gone to see Captain Knox at the Army Base and that my pre-induction physical had been set for May 7th. If I passed it, and there was no reason why I shouldn't, I could take some tests and go on to OTC. Captain Knox had been friendly, talking to me the way a doctor might during a routine office call. I hadn't had to stand at attention. In fact, he'd asked me to sit down right away. I think he treated me that way because I was Tim's nephew and Tim was his friend. During the half hour that we talked, I became convinced that OTC was the answer after all. No, you didn't need a wife, not at first anyway, and maybe not ever. The army was a man's world. Generals needed wives, but I wasn't going to be a general. I said, "I have a girl. What if we wanted to get married while I was in OTC?" And Captain Knox said, "We advise against that. Don't be hasty."

As soon as everything was settled, Tim had taken me out to dinner at The Shelton in Boston. "You made a good impression on Captain Knox," he told me. "He phoned and told me he thinks highly of you. He says you have the stuff. I have the feeling you're going to make us proud of you." It was the usual bullshit, but it made me feel good, because it does make you feel good to have the approval of your uncle, even if he is phony baloney. It also feels good to have the approval of your mother and of the people you work with. Since my boss, Frank DiPietro, was an old friend of hers, my mother could keep an eye on me by remote control. She phoned him once or twice to see how I was doing and his reports were positive. And I was a good busboy, too, efficient, polite, conscientious. I cared about filling those water glasses. I had a sharp eye out for those celebrities who needed another pat of unsalted butter. I was prompt with the Parker House rolls. I smiled, I was deferential, I learned to say "sir" with just the right intonation. Tim also said, "You know, it says in the Bible, 'Whatever your right hand finds to do, do it with all your might.' I know you're going to give OTC everything you've got. You're a winner, not a loser, and you're going to make it."

It was nice to be called a winner. "I will make it," I answered. And I meant it.

My hours at the Ritz were from eleven to three and from five to eight. During my afternoon break, from three to five, I would catch the MTA car out to Huntington Avenue, where I would run on the track at the Y. I'd decided to build up my body in preparation for the army. I also took a class in swimming. It met on Tuesdays and Thursdays, at nine in the morning. On those days I would arrive at the Ritz feeling refreshed, clean, ready for anything. Swimming was great. I was learning the six beat overhand crawl. Running was great, too. It opened me up, in my body and in my mind. It put me in touch with things in a way I hadn't been since I was on the track team in high school. But there was more.

We swam naked. Even the coach, a tanned, handsome man from Boston University, was naked. We had to perform lifesaving drills at the end of each session, which involved grasping another person around the chest and swimming with him to the other end of the pool. I always picked the same person—a dark, curly-haired young man, about my age—and I always got out of the pool with a half-hardon. The coach either didn't notice or thought it was a natural reaction to the rubbing and bumping involved in the lifesaving drill. I had no way of knowing, since nothing was ever said. The dark, curly-haired young man had a friend in the class. I saw them talking in the locker room once. They kept looking in my direction. The expression on the face of the young man was contemptuous. After that, I chose someone else to rescue, the least attractive man in the class. Then I didn't get a half-hardon. Then it was just a task you had to perform to pass the class. Then it was all right. No one looked at me contemptuously after that. But why? I wondered. When it was so exhilarating and energizing and sexually exciting to hold that curly-haired young man by the chest, with the palm of my right hand resting on his nipple, my fingers under his biceps, his head on my shoulder, his whole beautiful body brushing and bumping against mine in the water... What was wrong with it! It was beautiful. But the contemptuous look stayed with me. It registered. It was wrong to feel the way I felt. That was the message.

The dining room of the Ritz was blue and white, glittery. Tall windows looked out over the Public Garden. Everything from the plates to the silverware to the table linens glowed with a silvery light. But you changed your clothes in a locker room in the dank basement of the hotel under a single light bulb that hung from a cord. One morning, opening the door to the locker room, I saw two young men who worked in the kitchen, wrestling in a corner. It was more than wrestling! One of them shouted something in what I assumed to be Greek (all the boys in the kitchen were Greek immigrants) and they separated. They'd been bopping. The one on the bottom pushed the other away. He had a look on his face which was part excitement, part anger, part embarrassment. He was beautiful! Everything in me wanted to join them. But the game was over. Nor could I communicate with them, since neither one of them spoke English. They left and went up into the kitchen, laughing and chattering to each other.

Someday, I told myself, I was going to find someone who did not look at me contemptuously and who did speak English and I was going to do it with him, but where was he? I read in the papers that McCarthy had had thousands of government workers in Washington fired as suspected Communists (which really meant suspected queers) but that was Washington. Where were the queers in Boston? We were supposed to meet in bars, but where were the bars? Not that I could get into one anyway, since you had to be twenty-one. But I started looking in through the doors of bars as I walked in the city. All I saw were bent backs and how did a queer back differ from a back that wasn't queer? We were supposed to walk funny. We were supposed to wear jewelry and mascara. We were supposed to have high-pitched voices. We were supposed to be unable to whistle through our teeth. I took to watching the patrons in the Ritz bar. I could stand by the blue velvet drape and look in as I was on duty. I never saw anyone who walked funny or wore jewelry or mascara or talked with a high-pitched voice. And every man looked as if he could whistle through his teeth any time he wanted to. They looked about as queer as my Uncle Tim. So obviously wherever we hung out, it wasn't the Ritz bar. But where was it?

On Sunday afternoons, when the Y was closed, I walked in the Public Garden during my afternoon break. So, on the second Sunday in April, I left the Ritz by the kitchen entrance off an alley, crossed Arlington Street and entered the Garden. Boston was struggling toward spring, but at that moment it was an unequal struggle and it looked as if spring might lose. The wind was blustery, the sunshine came and went, the colors in the tulips were incandescent one minute and then non-existent the next. But when the clouds parted and let the light through, everything flashed into life—people, pigeons, the forsythia bushes along the iron fence. Everything vibrated with terrific energy. However, it never lasted for more than a minute or two. The sun would disappear behind the clouds again, it would feel chilly and faces that had looked momentarily happy... Well, when the sun went away, you could see the worried lines there. Everyone had been frowning all along.

On the Beacon Street side of the Garden, Father Feeney was preaching, surrounded by his disciples who were, in turn, surrounded by spectators. Feeney had been excommunicated from the Church for disobedience to his superiors, so now he preached here every Sunday in the open air. He'd formed his own group called "Servants of the Sacred Heart of Jesus," and they all lived together in a mansion in Brighton. He wore a black robe with a red heart on it and his disciples wore gray robes without hearts. He was the maddest of mad Irishmen with glaring, lunatic eyes, one of those Celtic jaws that jutted out like an iron railing, cheekbones as sharp as shoulder blades and lips as thin as razors. I probably had ancestors as mad as Feeney back in the Old Country, but, hopefully, we'd had sense enough to keep them tied by a rope in the woodshed. He gave me the creeps, but I always stopped to listen to him anyway. It was hard not to stop. He had such a powerful voice. It stopped you in your tracks, though everything he said was vicious and small-minded. Today he was talking about Julius and

Ethel Rosenberg. I heard the words "Jew Red spies" and "Commie traitors." I also heard him say, "Two thousand years ago, the Jews killed the Prophet." Then some guy in the crowd—probably a stooge, since Feeney planted his own hecklers in the crowd—yelled, "Profit? All the Jews care about is the profit!" And some people laughed. It was ugly laughter, dark and mean.

I decided to move on, because this kind of thing depressed me and why be depressed during my break? But then I saw Luanne standing on the edge of the crowd. She was wearing a big floppy hat (it was blowing around her head in the breeze) and sunglasses, but it was her all right. And this was the logical place for her to be on a Sunday afternoon. She lived right over there on Charles, so the Public Garden was her neighborhood park. I moved toward her. She didn't see me though until I said, "Hey! How are you!"

She turned, recognized me and cried out, "Steve! Steve, honey, where y' been?" Then she hugged me. I got wrapped up in her hat and coat. It felt good, being hugged by someone on the edge of all that fanatical hatred Feeney was preaching. It was like—defiance! You can hate, but we're going to hug! Like that! "They told me you quit. Why haven't you called me? It's been weeks!"

"My whole life has changed, Luanne. I got a new job and I'm going in the army. I even had a birthday since the last time I saw you. I'm twenty."

"Happy birthday!"

"Yeah, I'm gettin' up there." At that moment I noticed a little boy behind her. I knew it had to be her son. His thumb was in his mouth and his eyes were on me. Why was I hugging his mother that way? Who was this man? I could tell that this was what he was thinking. I was a threat to him. I said, "Hi, kid!" He didn't answer.

"Oh, this is my little boy Rafe," Luanne said. "He came up on the bus from New York yesterday. He isn't going to be living with his daddy anymore." She took him up in her arms. "You're going to live with Mommy now, aren't you, sweetheart?" She kissed him on the cheek. His eyes never left my face, though. He was a cute kid. His eyes were large and a rich chocolate brown. They held my attention. They were hypnotizing. He didn't look anything like his mother. He was dark. She was light. Well, now I was going to have to think of Luanne as a mother. It was strange. Well, of course, she'd been a mother all along, but... Here was the actual kid.

81

Feeney was shouting, "Communist dupes, Communist dupes!" A woman, probably not one of his plants, was screaming back at him, "Fascist Red-baiter! Anti-Semitic bigot!" Her face was distorted with rage. She was out of her head. It was like the Two Minutes Hate in *1984* except this wasn't happening on a telescreen. It was real. It was right here a few feet from us, in a real park, under real trees, on real newly minted spring grass with real tulips tossing in the wind.

"Let's get out of here," Luanne said, looking at me over the top of Rafe's head. "A little of this goes a long way."

We went to a children's playground, which had swings, slides, and a jungle gym, sat on a bench and watched Rafe play in a sandbox with some other children. Actually, he didn't play with the other children. He sat off to the side and watched them. They didn't invite him to join them. He didn't ask to be included. He just sat there, staring.

"That woman my ex-husband is living with in New York doesn't want Rafe around," Luanne said. "She's such a high-class bitch, she says Rafe cramps her style. Anyway, I like having him with me. I get ADC and Martin has to pay child support. So I'm a welfare mother now and I get free government surplus food, too, peanut butter, cooking oil, cheese, rice, pinto beans. The Agency will even pay for our counseling sessions with Dr. Stiller. He's a clinical psychologist at Boston University. We have an appointment for next Tuesday."

This playground was in an enclosed place scooped out of a hillside. It was warmer here because we were out of the wind. We were fenced in, with these kids. Their mothers were in here, too, some of them in advanced stages of pregnancy, sitting on other benches, chatting to each other. Mostly their eyes were on their kids, but sometimes they looked at us. They weren't friendly looks. They weren't hostile looks. They were just looks. Did they think we were husband and wife? Probably not. Adulterous lovers sneaking a few minutes here on a Sunday afternoon? My guess was that men never came into this place. So I was a curiosity. Where were the husbands of these women? Home watching baseball on TV?

Luanne saw me staring at one of the pregnant women and said, "I call this place Ovary Park. Even on cold days, it's warm in here. It's all that maternal heat."

"If I wasn't sitting here, I suppose the women would come over to talk to you, right?"

"Oh, no. I'm too unconventional for them. They can see I don't belong. So, no, they wouldn't come over."

Luanne looked like any other woman to me. Why would they think she was unconventional? She even had her kid with her. "What is it, your hat?"

"Well, yes, the hat's part of it. But even without the hat, they'd know. I don't belong. It would take too long to explain. Women know. It's a female thing. Animal instinct. Even if they did include me, I don't want to talk about diaper services and formula, and that's what they're interested in right now. And I'm divorced. That makes me a threat."

"How would they know you're divorced?"

"I have that look. They know. I'm not their cup of Lipton's. And they're not mine."

Rafe left the sandbox and came over to us. His eye had never really left me—this strange man sitting on a bench next to his mother—and I'd been conscious of his wariness, his suspicion as I sat there. Now he climbed up next to his mother and said, "I wanna go home. I don' wanna be out here when they roll up the sidewalks."

She took him in her lap. "I told him Boston is such a hick town compared to New York, they roll up the sidewalks at five o'clock. I'm going to have to watch my tongue. Rafe, honey, we'll go home when Simon comes. Simon's going to meet us here, remember?" She stroked his dark curly hair. He looked as if he might go to sleep there in her lap. It was nice. It was a nice thing to witness. "Simon's my new boyfriend," she explained.

"Oh, I see."

"He's happily married and has a lovely three year old daughter. He drives a truck. He's great in bed."

"And he's happily married? Doesn't it bother him, cheating on his wife?"

"It doesn't seem to. Why? I've never noticed that it did."

"Well, it could bother him in his subconscious, where you can't see it."

"Sub-conscious! Honey, Simon doesn't even have a conscious. He's totally numb between the ears. I like it that way. I'm through with sensitive men."

I recognized the emotion that ripped through me as jealousy. That was ridiculous. I wasn't going to play dog in the manger, snapping at the cows who came in to feed.

Luanne went on. "There's something I should tell you before you meet Simon. When he was in the navy, he was in a bad accident. He was thirty-six hours on the operating table. They had to rebuild his face. Don't act surprised when you see his face. It's the plastic surgery."

"Where did you meet him?"

"In the Beacon Bar," she answered.

"When's Simon comin'?" Rafe asked, looking up at his mother.

"Soon," Luanne said.

A child fell off a swing. He cried out. His mother lumbered toward him, her maternity dress billowing out like a big white sail around her. She held him and comforted him. The other mothers had been alerted by the cry, but they remained on their benches. It was all biological, all basic. Being queer might be a phase you passed in and out of (though I didn't believe that anymore) but having kids was forever. I'd never have a son. I'd never know any of this. Since it looked as if this was all there was to life, what was my life going to be like? Luanne was watching my face. "How did your mother act toward you when you were growing up?" she asked.

"Like what?"

"Loving, cruel, hostile? What do you remember?"

"I used to read a lot. Books from the library. Kids' books. One day I came home and she'd returned them all. Where the books had been, there was a fielder's glove. She said, 'Get your ass to the city park now!'"

"Was that traumatic?"

"Was it what? No, it was the best thing she could have done for me. I finally made friends. I met my friend Ro there. He taught me how to field a ball. I got good at it, too. I learned to be good at it because he was a good teacher and I enjoyed being with him. Then I had a gang I ran with. I loved that. I was happy. I was a happy kid. My mother did me a favor. She pushed me into life. I wish that phase of my life could have gone on forever. Do girls go through phases like that, growing up?"

"Oh, some do. Slumber parties, crushes on movie stars, dances. I never went through it, but I watched other girls who did."

"You didn't belong?"

"Never. St. Charles, Missouri rejected me from the start. Little Phyllis Dusinberre simply did not belong."

"Who's 'Phyllis Dusinberre?' Oh! Your name..."

"Honey, if you were born 'Phyllis Dusinberre' wouldn't you change your name to Luanne as soon as you could? And then I married a guy named Hanks. At the time that seemed better than 'Dusinberre.' But later I wasn't so sure."

I looked up. A man who could only be Simon had entered the enclosure. Some of the mothers looked up, too, mildly interested. He saw us but he didn't come over right away. Luanne's back was toward him. She didn't know he was there.

"Do you think I could get some counseling from this Stiller guy?" I asked. "There are some questions I want to ask him."

"What questions?"

"Well, it seems to me that if you're... I mean, if..." I couldn't say the word. It would ring in every mother's ear like an alarm buzzer. But then I did say it. "If you're queer, there's only one question, 'Why?' I keep asking 'Why?' and the only answer I get is 'No one knows!' Maybe Stiller knows."

Simon was approaching us. Luanne had been right about his face. Interest quickened among the mothers. Was this guy the husband? The angry lover? The rival? The real father of the child?

Luanne saw Simon. Her face changed.

"C'mon," he said, ignoring me. "I'm late."

She didn't want to be rushed though. She was in no hurry. She didn't get up. "I'm talking to my friend," she said.

"O.K.," he said and walked away.

"Oh, my God," Luanne said. "Goodbye, Steve. Call me!" Rafe tumbled off her lap. She ran after Simon. Rafe ran along behind her. A second later I was alone in the enclosure with the mothers. I could hear Luanne and Simon arguing on the other side of the fence. I heard Rafe wailing. I realized that each mother was writing her own script in her mind, putting it all in order, making it comprehensible. And every one of them had it wrong.

8

I'm sitting here at my Apple computer, an instrument I could not have dreamed of in 1954, writing my book. It is 5:10 A.M., May 12, 1989. I am looking at a greeting card which Luanne gave me 35 years ago. The card has survived Joseph R. McCarthy, Roy Cohn, Dwight David Eisenhower, Senator Millard E. Tydings, Judge Dorothy Kenyon, Senator Pat McCarran, Cardinal Spellman, Adlai Stevenson, Everett McKinley Dirksen and both my parents. The envelope is addressed this way: DEAREST ONE—STEVE RILEY. The card itself shows a cartoon figure with a dark smudge for a body. Two cartoon arms hang down on either side of the smudge. They are not attached to the smudge. Two legs with bare feet are drawn in below the smudge. They are not attached either. The face consists of a large ovoid nose, eyes with dark marks under them, hair hanging down around what would be the outline of the face if the outline had been drawn in. It hasn't been. The figure is frowning. To the left of the head are the words: IF THINGS LOOK BLACK— Opening the card, I see that the interior is black. These words are printed in white: —IT'S ONLY BECAUSE THEY ARE!

Luanne has signed it, "A chick who knows."

*

"Sons?"

It was about ten o'clock on a rainy April night. Brian and I had been out for a beer. I was now twenty years old and I looked all of sixteen. But we had found a tavern where the bartender never asked me for an I.D. Coming into the kitchen, wet and dripping, we saw our father at the table. We sat down with him. Outside, the rain drummed down, boom, boom, boom against the windows.

"Sons, your mother saw the doctor today about her 'female troubles,'" my father said. "She's going to have to go into Boston City hospital next week to get herself fixed up. It's what they call a… I forget what they call it."

"Hysterectomy?" Brian said.

"Yes, that's it. She'll be all right. It's a routine operation. They do them all the time. But she won't be able to work for a while after it's over, so there'll be that much less money coming into the house."

Brian got up, went to the cupboard and took down three glasses and a bottle of whiskey. I shook my head, no. I didn't want whiskey. My father looked as if he did want it—even needed it—but he considered and then shook his head, no. He couldn't have it. He knew where that route led. Brian poured himself a shot. A second later I saw that he'd drained the glass. He said, "The three of us are working. We'll make out. We've always made out in the past. We survive. We do O.K."

"Yes," my father said. "We're survivors."

A few minutes before, in the bar, Brian had said, "I'm going to tell Tim to take his job and shove it!" But I could see now that he was thinking it over. He was never going to be able to tell Tim to shove it. He was never going to be able to tell anyone to shove it. He was trapped. "Sure, Dad. We always manage somehow. Don't worry about it."

But my father said, "Medical expenses are terrible. You don't know. Insurance only covers part of it. It's money. It's always money. It's money every minute of your life. You never get out from under till the day you die. Your mother and myself, we're going to be living here alone after you two leave, trying to get by on what I make with Sunny Orange, which, God knows, isn't much. I worry, that's all. I worry all the time. And what if I get sick and can't work?"

We talked for an hour and then went to bed. I fell asleep right away, but I woke up a few hours later because Brian was tossing around in his bunk under mine, calling out in his sleep. I climbed down and shook him by the shoulder. He came awake very slowly. "You were yelling in your sleep, Brian," I said.

"I was having a terrible dream."

"Yeah, you were yelling. You woke me up."

"It's this Tim business. It's tearing me apart. It's keeping me from getting the sleep I need."

I decided to make a joke of it. "Yeah, it's keeping me from getting the sleep I need, too."

But Brian snapped back at me, "It's not funny to me!"

Being snapped at that way hurt my feelings and made me angry, but I could see his point. If he said yes, he'd be Tim's flunky for the rest of his life. If he said no, he'd betray everyone—his father, his mother, his new wife. I was glad I didn't have any decisions like that to make. I'd seen Captain Knox just the way I was supposed to and now everything was settled for me. But for Brian opportunity had knocked but when he'd opened the door there'd been a gunman there ready to take him prisoner.

*

Luanne managed to get fired from Pawtucket Paper Box, so that she could live on unemployment and spend more time with her child. Simon was on the road a lot with his truck, but even if this hadn't been true, he wouldn't have been able to spend much time with Luanne, because he had a wife. So I began to spend my free time with Luanne and Rafe, going to foreign films, to the Museum of Fine Arts, to a concert at Symphony Hall. I began to keep a diary, like Winston Smith in *1984*. Opening that diary now—it's a spiral ring notebook which cost me thirty-five cents and not the "thick, quarto-sized blank book with the red back, marbled cover and smooth creamy paper a little yellowed by age" that Winston found in the frowsy little junk shop in a slummy quarter of London—I see that I made a list: "Alec Guinness, Modigliani, Schubert, Dylan Thomas, Aldous Huxley, D.H. Lawrence..." My education had begun.

Rafe was a problem. He'd wander off, even though we both did our best to watch him, and we'd find him in some remote gallery about to topple a three thousand year old statue from Crete or to smear chocolate on a Van Gogh. Once we found him in a broom closet near the Egyptian Room trying to open a container of cleaning fluid. Luanne got him into a nursery school. But then the people who ran the school began to put pressure on her. She showed me a pamphlet they'd given her, *A Guide for Parents of Gifted Children*. They had decided that Rafe was gifted. "Listen to this," she said, holding up the pamphlet. "'Do you answer your child's questions with patience and good humor?' Yesterday he asked me a question and I just screamed at him. I probably traumatized him for life. 'Do you provide opportunities for decision-making by your child with follow-up of learning to evaluate decisions after carrying out whatever action was taken?'

Whoever wrote that wasn't gifted. What do you suppose it means? 'Do you find places where he can study and work at his hobbies?' I know what that means. It means I should be living in a ten-room house in suburbia. He gets a corner of my bedroom and the closet. What else have I got? 'Do you provide a place to display his work?' He did a mural with crayons on the bathroom wall. 'Do you take him on trips to points of interest where he can express his inner life?' Of course! I took him to see Stiller. Stiller put him in a room with a teddy bear. He said, 'Rafe, this bear is your Mommy.' Then we watched through one of those special windows as Rafe tore the bear to pieces. Stiller turned to me and said, 'Well, Mrs. Hanks, I think extensive counseling is called for, don't you?' Steve, what am I going to do?"

"Well, this is the hand you've been dealt. Play it out."

And maybe the kid really was gifted! One day he turned to me and said, staring up at me with those large chocolate-brown eyes, "Do souls have dreams like people do?" And all I could say was, "Oh, wow." What planet was this kid living on inside that beautiful head? Where was he coming from? Where had he been?

I did what I could to help, picking him up at nursery school, taking him to the playground, babysitting. He seemed to like me and I didn't mind playing daddy. How many opportunities would I have for that in my life anyway? One afternoon, during my afternoon break from the Ritz, we three sat on a park bench and watched the crazy people walk by. I was holding Rafe in my lap. His head was under my chin and I could smell his hair. Kid's hair doesn't smell like adult hair. Luanne said, after an old lady had walked by shouting obscenities, "I think ninety-five percent of these people are certifiably insane. And yet, every fifth or sixth person is beautiful and that person is always a man. Why is that?"

"It's their inner confidence," I said. "It comes out through the way they walk. It's beautiful. It's a magic men have when they feel good about their bodies."

"And the women seem so shut down," Luanne said.

"I like to watch men because I'm a man myself. I love my own body, so I like to watch men's bodies. My body just flows toward their bodies. It's automatic. It's like biology. It's sexual. But then..."

"Then what?"

"Well, then I get this look sometimes—hostile, contemptuous. So I just draw up into myself like a snail. I feel this glow and then I get a slap in the face. My body has a way of thinking its own thoughts and they're beautiful. But then it gets slapped down. If bodies could just be allowed to go along on their own, things would be fine. But there's this... What is it? Social conditioning? My body's right. But the conditioning is all wrong. Do you know what I mean?"

Luanne said, "Oh, Steve." Then she put her head on my shoulder. It was very tender. We communicated like that sometimes. After a minute of this, I got up, we said goodbye and hugged and I went back to work at the Ritz. It was good to have a woman friend. On some levels, we understood each other. We really did. I'd always heard you couldn't have a friendship with a woman, but that was bullshit. So much of what they told me was bullshit. I was thinking it all through, discarding the bullshit. It felt good.

I could express these thoughts sitting on a park bench with Luanne and Rafe, drawing on the protective coloration they provided. Alone in South Boston, it was a different matter. One afternoon at Carson Beach, I saw some words written on a wall: KILL KIKES! Those words had been crossed out and someone else had written, using a different color paint: KILL NIGGERS! Those words had been crossed out, too, and a third person had written, KILL QUEERS! That hadn't been crossed out. While I stood there, staring at the words on the wall, my body began to shrink. It went cold. I could feel my testicles turning to ice. Someone wanted to kill me. Who? Far, far down the beach a man was moving toward me. Maybe it was him! How would he do it, with a gun, a knife, a rope? Would he hit me from behind without warning? How could I protect myself? I shouldn't be out here without a weapon. I stared at the words: KILL QUEERS! That was me. I was queer. I could be killed. I had a couple of hours free. I'd find a hardware store. I'd get a can of black paint. I'd paint over all the words. I set out to do that, but before I got off the beach I saw some more of it: JEW BASTARDS DIE! And then HOMOS DIE! And then I realized that even if I spent the rest of my life painting over words like these, I'd never get the job finished. They were always out there ahead of me, writing it in faster than I could cancel it. Hatred was stronger than love. And yet... I couldn't seem to stop loving! It just came natural to me. It was the way I was. I couldn't control it. It flowed out of me automatically. It was a problem I had, something I definitely had to work on.

*

Luanne did get me an appointment with Stiller. It was on my day off. On the same day, at ten in the morning, my mother underwent surgery at Boston City Hospital. As I was seeing a psychologist about my mind, she was seeing a surgeon about her body. I had agreed to meet my father and brother in a bar on Albany Street, a block from the hospital, after my session was over. Of course, I didn't tell them I was seeing a psychologist. From the bar, we could walk to the hospital to visit my mother. I'd told Luanne that I'd stop by to see her later, because she was interested in what Stiller would tell me. She'd told me, "Stiller won't give you advice. He'll be cool, professional. This isn't psychiatry. That takes years. It's counseling. Don't expect miracles. It's just a way to get things off your chest."

Stiller's office was in one of those beautiful old 19th Century mansions on Bay State Road, one of the buildings Boston University had acquired for offices. Luanne had been wrong about Stiller. He wasn't cool. He wasn't impersonal. As soon as he saw me, he seemed to hate me. He had a little red moustache. It twitched. His eyes jumped behind his glasses. His lips came together as if he'd bitten into something sour. I told him my name, wondering if he was confusing me with someone he didn't like, some client who'd offended him in some way. But no. He was expecting me. "Riley, Steve," he said. O.K., so that wasn't it. "I can give you twenty-five minutes. What's your problem?" I was standing at the open window. I could hear crew members chanting on the Charles River. My problem was, if I could get into that narrow racing boat with them, I'd do it with every one of them. But why? Not "Why would that be a problem?" But "Why them!" Why not some sophomore from Radcliffe instead? Why was I the way I was?

I sat down in the chair provided for clients. As I looked across at Stiller, I could see how tired he was. It was all there in his face—the black marks under the eyes, the pale skin, the lines around the mouth. He had a terrible job here, listening to people's problems all day. I almost felt sorry for him. If he'd been nicer, I might have worked up some real sympathy for him. "My problem is, I had intercourse with a woman and nothing happened."

"So?"

"To me, nothing happened."

"And?"

His fatigue must have been bone deep. I could see that. I wanted to get up and walk out of there but, what the hell! I might as well go through with it! After all, I was here. And Luanne had gone to a lot of trouble to get me in. "And I want to know something," I said. "No, wait. I already know. I mean, I know I'm attracted to members of my own sex. I just want clarification. I knew about my sexual attraction toward men before I had relations with this woman, but I knew it in a different way. What I'm wondering is... Well, why am I the way I am? What made me this way? What made me, well... What made me queer?"

"We know very little about them," Stiller answered. "The longest we've been able to keep one under observation is twenty months." He handled the words "them" and "one" the way an overly fastidious person might handle underwear that's been dropped on the floor by a stranger. "But we do know this. They don't have sexual relations with women. If you're one of the homosexual group, how do you explain the fact that you did?"

"They never have sexual relations with women?"

"They have sexual relations with men. You had sexual relations with a woman. What makes you think you're homosexual? It seems to me your problem is a heterosexual problem. So why did you have sexual relations with a woman if you're homosexual?"

"It was expected of me," I answered.

"Who expected it of you?"

"Everybody! That's all I ever heard, growing up. 'Get a woman and screw her!' 'Get laid!' 'Lose your cherry!' I just fell into it. I didn't stop to think. That's a problem with me. I never stop to think."

"But you've thought about it since."

"I've thought about it a lot since."

"Well, so much for women. How many men have you had sexual relations with?"

"How do you mean?"

"I'd rather not go into specifics. I'll leave that up to you."

"Do you mean, 'Have I been to bed with a man?'"

"Look, Mr. Riley, I'm on a tight schedule here. I haven't got time for games. Why don't you just answer my question?"

"I've never been to bed with a man."

"How many homosexuals do you know?"

"I don't know any."

"Say that again."

"What? That I don't know any? What's wrong? Do you think I'm lying to you?"

"People have been known to. This woman, was she a prostitute?"

"No!"

92

"Tell me about your sexual fantasies. What do you think about when you masturbate?"

"This is hard to talk about. But I always think about men. I can put women in my fantasies, but I can't keep them there. To be honest, I stopped trying to put them in my fantasies when I was about fifteen years old. It was too much trouble. It didn't work. It never worked."

"And what do you do with the men?"

"Oh, this is hard! I hold them. We hold each other. We touch each other. Look, this isn't easy for me! We... We just love each other."

"If those are your fantasies, they're very rare. You should know that true homosexuals have fantasies very different from yours."

"What are their fantasies like?"

He didn't answer.

But I persisted. "I want to know," I said.

He wasn't going to tell me though. Instead, he said, "You have a lot of growing up to do. You show a remarkable degree of immaturity. Your fantasies are the fantasies of a boy who has just entered puberty. How old are you?"

"I'm twenty."

"You have the fantasies of a boy of twelve. They may be normal in a boy of twelve, but it's time you outgrew them."

His secretary opened the door and looked in. "The Rogers boy phoned and cancelled. Can you work the Phillips girl in? I moved that Maguire person up to the three-fifteen spot. And do you want me to call Kingsley to tell him there's an opening?" Christ, the whole town was trying to get in to see this guy! Stiller rattled something off to the secretary and she closed the door. I looked around the room. It was just a sterile space consecrated to mental suffering. I could still hear the crew members chanting. They were out there on the bright blue water in the spring sunshine. They were in touch with their bodies. They weren't experiencing mental pain. I wanted to be with them. I wanted to be running or swimming. I knew what mental health was. It was in a healthy body. It wasn't in this room.

Stiller wrote something on a pad. Then he said, "This woman you tried to have intercourse with is someone you know personally, then. It's not a woman you hired for the night?"

"It's a friend."

"Are you still in touch with her?"

"Yeah. I see her almost every day."

"Was she receptive to intercourse?"

"Yeah. She was receptive."

"Then, Mr. Riley, I suggest you try again."

"I don't want to try again. Once was enough."

"If you had had successful sexual relations with this woman, would that have made a difference in your evaluation of yourself?"

"How do you mean?"

"Would you still feel that you are a member of the homosexual group?"

"I'd still be attracted to members of my own sex."

"Yes, but if you had satisfactory sexual relations with a woman once, you could have them twice, three times. You'd then have a heterosexual orientation. If I'd failed only once, I'd try it again. You might succeed a second time. Wouldn't that solve your problem? If you failed your driver's test once, wouldn't you try it again?"

"It's not a driver's test."

"No. But we are what we do. If you performed successfully as a heterosexual, you could think of yourself as a heterosexual and the problem would be solved. You could marry and have children."

"I don't want to marry and have children. I'm attracted to men."

"Well, some men, aware that they possess deviant traits, but unwilling, for social, moral or religious reasons, to indulge them, live alone and make a thoroughly adequate adjustment to society. If you refuse to marry, you can live alone. You have that option."

"I don't want to live alone."

"Why not?"

"Because there's no love in that."

"I need to ask you how you know you're homosexual."

"Well, I know it in my mind."

"In other words, it's a thought. If it's in your mind, it has to be a thought, correct?"

"Yes. It's a thought and it's in my mind."

"Thoughts can be changed. If you had the thought in your mind that you were a heterosexual, you'd be a heterosexual. Is that correct?"

"I suppose so. But I don't have that thought in my mind."

"You don't have it in your mind at this moment. But that doesn't mean you won't have it in your mind six months or a year from now. Do you still believe the things you believed when you were five? Do you still believe in Santa Claus? Beliefs change. You can change your belief that you are a homosexual. Work on it. Begin by trying sexual intercourse with your woman friend one more time."

"Well, I know it in my body, too."

"Where in your body? Which part of your body? Your liver? Your heart? Are you saying your body doesn't change? In seven years, every cell in your body changes. Excuse me, but you can't know it in your body. That's just something your mind is telling you. Your problem is mental. You have an obsession. It's related to stress. Try again. If you were thrown from a horse, wouldn't you get right back on and ride again? If you try again and succeed, the problem will resolve itself immediately."

"I'm not going to try again."

"Well, you're going to have a difficult time in life if you continue to think of yourself as a member of the homosexual group. You'll have trouble getting a job. Even if you get one, you'll have trouble keeping one. All the other people working with you will be married. You'll stand out. If you go into law or medicine or government, you'll be expected to marry. You could be an artist or a dress designer. People are more tolerant of artists and dress designers. But otherwise, how do you intend to make a living? If you indulge your sexual desires, you'll have problems with the police. You can be taken to court, jailed. You can be blackmailed. You won't be allowed to do any type of work which involves a security clearance. You won't be able to enlist in the military. Does marriage or a celibate life seem more attractive to you now, Mr. Riley?"

"Why can't I enlist in the military?" I asked, frightened.

"You didn't know that?"

"I heard they take you in a room and ask you if you like women. I don't dislike women. I was going to say, 'I like women,' that's all."

"There's a question on the form you're required to fill out before you take the physical examination. It asks you if you have homosexual tendencies. You're required to answer yes or no."

"What happens if I answer yes?"

"You're cut out of the herd, so to speak. A psychologist talks to you in private. If it's confirmed that you have these tendencies, you're not inducted. There's no social stigma attached to this. You're not classified as homosexual. You're simply not inducted. The whole matter is kept confidential."

"I'll have to lie!"

"Well, yes, you can lie. Some men do, I'm sure. But if you lie and enter the military and then have sexual relations with a man, you'll be court-martialed and given a dishonorable discharge. I can't believe you don't know all this."

"I didn't know all this."

"Well, you've learned something. Good. Now I worked you in at the request of Mrs. Hanks, and I did it as special favor to her, but I had to juggle appointments, I have a dozen people waiting, so if you would... Do you need help? Are you all right? Can you stand?"

I couldn't get up from the chair. I felt divorced from my body. I was afraid that if I got up, my legs wouldn't support me. I could still hear the crew members chanting on the river, but what had seemed beautiful minutes before was now dark and threatening and dangerous. If I lied and entered the military, even to look at a man would be an offense. And I'd be surrounded by men every minute of the day. But not to go in... Oh, my mother! My uncle! "What choice do I have?" I whispered.

Stiller had come around the desk and was lifting me gently by my right arm. "That's for you to decide," he said. "It's up to you. No one can make the decision for you. But if I've helped you in any way to come to a decision... Well, that's what I'm here for. And I'm glad you came in."

Just before I walked into the bar on Albany Street where I was to meet my father and brother, a panhandler stepped up beside me and said, "Y' got any spare change?" You think of panhandlers as broken-down winos with toothless mouths and grey stubble on their faces, but this was a kid my own age. He had a Boston Braves baseball cap on his head. He was wearing a torn sweatshirt and dungarees and sneakers. "I haven't eaten all day."

Oh, man! Poor son of a bitch. I reached into the pocket of my peacoat. I had thirty-five cents. I put it into his hand. "Here, go eat, for crissake!" I said. My hand touched the palm of his hand. His fingers closed over the coins. There were hunks of red-gold hair sticking out around the baseball cap. He was wearing glasses held together by a piece of adhesive tape. He thanked me and walked off toward the crowd on Massachusetts Avenue. I watched him disappear into that crowd. I was going to disappear into that crowd very soon, because I was a man with no future.

Once inside, I went to the bar and ordered a ginger ale. I told the bartender, "I told my father and brother I'd meet them in here." I didn't want any trouble. I knew I looked like a sixteen year old kid. It was a tough, ugly, dark bar. I had no proof of age. The television flickered on a shelf up above. McCarthy, McCarthy. Flash. Welch, flash, flash, a guy named Juliana. Cohn. Schine, Cohn, cropped photographs, flash. It just went on forever. There was no end to it. It was all coming out of The Ministry of Truth and they were doing it to control men's minds. It was Oceania. It really was. This was *1984!* No question about it. And there was Winston Smith at the end of the bar, head down over a drink, probably Victory Gin, looking like he'd just been let out of the Ministry of Love that morning. I went to a booth and sat down. I was still in shock.

Yes, in shock. My body registered it. What was I going to do? Tim had said, "You're a young man with no future!" And he'd held out a future to me. I hadn't slapped his hand away. I'd said, "O.K. Great! I'll do it!" And I'd gone through with it. So he approved of me. My mother approved of me. Everyone approved of me. And that felt good. I was no juvenile delinquent. I was no hood, hanging out on the corner, drinking Smoky Pete. I was a responsible human being. I was going to OTC. And now this. Five words on a form. "Do you have homosexual tendencies?" Of course I did. What Ministry had that question come from! Well, so you lied. Everyone lied. I'd lie. That's how they controlled you, they got you to lie. They knew you were lying and they wanted the control that the lie would give them. So I'd go in, riding on the waves of approval from my family, but with an inner dread in my body. Because I'd meet someone. I'd meet someone I liked. I knew that now. And when the moment came, I wasn't going to say no. Because I wasn't Saint Stevie living in a cave in the desert on honey and locusts. I wasn't some skin and bones ascetic in a hair shirt, lacerating myself with cactus spines. I was a man, with skin, muscles, nerves, bones, lips, cock, balls, ass. I didn't hate my body. I loved my body. But the army would own every cell of that body. Every time I blinked, my eyelids would register GOVERNMENT ISSUE as they rose and fell. Every flicker would register the fact that they owned my eyelids. They'd own my eyes, too. They'd even own my tear ducts and God help me if they functioned! They'd own my wrists, which could never even dream of going limp, not even for one single second. They'd own my larynx. If a single shriek ever came up out of that voice box, it was the stockade for Little Stevie. And they'd own my hands, which could never even dream of stroking another man's body. They'd own my lips, so I could never kiss another man. They'd own the tips of my fingers and my elbows and my knees. And they'd own my cock, so all personal pleasure would be in cold storage for the duration of my enlistment. I wouldn't even be able to jack off. They'd own my dreams. What if I cried out in my sleep in the barracks, "Ro, damn it, I did love you!" Who's this "Ro" character? "Ralph, all I ever wanted was to hold you naked under a blanket! Your ass, your sweet cock!" There'd be a hundred guys in the barracks, two hundred ears open to my dreams. I wouldn't dare to dream. I'd be afraid to fall asleep at night. And they'd get weekend passes so they could go out to fuck the whores. "Hey, Steve! Ain't y' comin' with us!"

When Brian finally came in, he didn't see me sitting in the booth in the dark. There was bright sunlight outside and your eyes had to adjust to the gloom when you stepped inside. I asked myself, "If Brian wasn't my brother, and he stepped into a bar this way, would I be sexually attracted to him?" I stared at him. There was an aura around his body from the sunlight pouring through the door. He was wearing a blue windbreaker, tan chinos and a white shirt and tie. He'd just come from work. Where the chinos hung over his cock there was that seductive little bulge, that hint of mystery, that energy center pulsating from the crotch. Everything was centered there. Everything radiated outward from that center—thoughts, desires, dreams, motivations, visions, futures! He walked over to the bar. He joked with the bartender. He ordered a drink. His clothes didn't really fit him. He didn't care about clothes. He just got dressed in the morning to avoid being arrested for nudity on the street. And his relationship with his body was problematical. It had let him down early. He'd been sick. He'd had to watch it all his life. It could betray him at any moment. He lived in an uneasy truce with it. No, I decided. I didn't want to do it with my brother.

The bartender said something to Brian and nodded in my direction. Brian saw me, came over and slid into the seat across from me. "Hey, Stevie! Been waitin' long?" Nor was Brian sexually attractive close up. He was just my brother, thin, nervous, quick, with a characteristic aggressive defensiveness thrown up to protect himself from other people. He was like a thousand other Irish-American young men walking the streets of Boston at that moment or riding the subways, hanging from a strap, reading the *Record-American,* or staring out through the windows of drugstores or office buildings. He was smiling though. He looked like a cat who'd gotten some cream. So I knew. I just knew. He'd made his decision.

"Hey, you decided, didn't you? You did, didn't you? I can tell."

"Yeah," he answered. "I called Tim an hour ago from the drugstore. I told him I'd be honored to work with him. I thanked him for the opportunity. He was real nice to me. Maybe he's not such a bad guy after all. I mean, he tries. I wonder now, why was I fighting it? I was acting like a kid. This is the chance of a lifetime. I almost blew it, too. But I finally came to my senses. Everything's falling into place, Stevie. I saw Mary today, too, at lunch, and we went to look at what they call a 'garden apartment' on Dartmouth. It's only four rooms, but it's nice. I feel good. I feel real good."

I was looking at his hands, his fingers, the wedding ring on the third finger of the left hand. I'd heard Mary say to my mother, "Our rings are gold, silver and rose gold. They symbolize the physical, the spiritual, the emotional." It was a symbol. It was important. It was his life. They'd bought them at Zale's, after not finding what they wanted at three other jewelry stores. He'd paid cash. They'd been saving for it. "Well, I'm glad it's settled, Brian. You're better off than I am. I have to make this decision about the army."

"What? I thought that was all taken care of!" He looked at me sharply.

"No, it's not taken care of... I don't want to talk about it, O.K.?"

"What's the matter? You sick?"

"No. I'm fine. I'll be all right."

"What are you drinkin' there, Stevie? It looks like soda water!"

"Ginger ale."

"Ginger ale! In this bar? Stevie, you're probably the only guy who ever ordered ginger ale in this place since they opened a hundred years ago. I'm gonna get you a man's drink! You're gonna celebrate my success with me. I'm gonna be in management. Me, a manager! Think of that! Now what do you want to drink? I'll get it for you! They don't care how old you are in here, Stevie! If you were in diapers, they'd serve you in here. Now what do you want?"

"Victory Gin," I answered.

Brian got me a whiskey and a glass of water for a chaser. Apparently you didn't order gin in here. In here, gin was feminine. You ordered whiskey. You drank it straight. You chased it with tap water. That was masculine. We sat there in the booth. I saw my father come in. He didn't see us. Brian didn't see him, since his back was to the door. My father was carrying flowers wrapped in green paper. I watched him, his stance, his way of walking. He belonged in here. This was his home territory, his turf. Good old Jack Riley! He'd know what to order. He wouldn't make any mistakes! When he came over, though, he had a cup of steaming hot coffee. He was an alcoholic. He was going to see his wife in the hospital. He couldn't take chances. In his body, alcohol was poison. It could kill him. They kept a pot of coffee brewing all day behind the bar for men like my father, and there were thousands of men like him. It was genetic. It was part of being Irish. You inherited this. I looked narrowly at Brian. I wondered.

"She'll be comin' out from under the ether now," my father said. "We can go up there in a half hour. I talked to the doctor on the phone. He said it was a routine operation and she did real well. She's gonna be O.K. She'll be fine. She's a strong woman and she's gonna come through it fine." He unzipped his Sunny Orange windbreaker. It said Sunny Orange on it right over the pocket with the snap on it. Under the windbreaker, he was wearing a blue work shirt. It said Sunny Orange on it, too. My father was owned by Sunny Orange. My father was owned by a lot of things. "I want you kids to be especially nice to her. Here. I bought these. I want you to hand them to her, Stevie. It'll mean a lot."

He handed me the flowers. I knew the names of these flowers. It wasn't masculine to know the names of flowers. But I knew the names of the flowers. My father could walk in here carrying flowers and it was O.K. I wouldn't have dared. I put the flowers next to my glass of whiskey. "This flower here," I said. "It's called babies'-breath."

"Well, it don't matter what you call 'em," my father said. "It's the thought that counts."

Maybe we were all alcoholics! I'd see. I'd test it. I'd get a second whiskey. I'd walk to the bar and order it myself. I didn't need Brian. I was a man! I stalked up to the bar, imitating my father's walk. It didn't work. I'm not my father. I'm myself! "I want a whiskey," I said to the bartender. He had a face like a prize-fighter's. Maybe he was a prize-fighter. It was that kind of bar.

I waited while he got the bottle. My eye was on the television. They were still arguing about that cropped photograph. This had been going on for weeks. Everybody knew that McCarthy and Cohn had cropped the photograph. Why did they go on and on this way, day after day, week after week? All of a sudden the Welch guy got a funny look on his face and leered, "Did you think this came from a pixie?" Everyone at the hearings laughed. It came across loud and clear. "Where did you think this picture I hold in my hand came from?" Then McCarthy flashed on—the jaw, the teeth, the beady eyes. He said, "Will that question be reread?" Oh Jesus! Someone reread it. I heard it again. "'Did you think this came from a pixie?'" McCarthy turned to Welch. He said. "Would counsel, for my benefit, define—I think he might be an expert on this—the word 'pixie'?"

Then Welch replied, "I should say, Mr. Senator, that a pixie is a close relative of a fairy."

The bartender was pushing the whiskey toward me across the bar. My eyes were riveted to the television screen. I didn't move. I didn't take the whiskey. They were laughing now at the hearings in Washington. It was derisive, mocking laughter. There was a lot of it. It went on for a long time. Then Welch said, getting the knife in, twisting it. "Shall I proceed, sir? Have I enlightened you?"

He'd beaten him! The Welch guy had beaten him! He'd won! I couldn't believe it. But he'd done it by calling him a fairy. He'd told the millions of people watching, "This guy's queer!" And McCarthy was finished, just like that! I paid the bartender, but I felt like a ghost—no body, no feeling. It was automatic, because... Because I just wasn't there any more. Because, look! Even McCarthy could get it! Call anybody a queer and you could destroy them in an instant! It was incredible!

McCarthy himself knew it. The camera had zeroed in on his big dark ugly face. He was getting his! Big Brother had struck! He tried to smile. It didn't work. Everybody knew now. He was through. "As I said," he said. Then he repeated it. "As I said, I think you might be an authority on what a pixie is." But McCarthy was the authority on what a pixie was because McCarthy was a pixie and everyone knew it and they were moving in for the kill now. I turned away. The glass of whiskey dropped out of my hand and bounced across the sawdust on the floor. I just stood there, staring down. From the television, you could hear the laughter. It was a snarling, vindictive, animal sound. It went on and on.

*

101

My mother was sitting up in bed, propped up by pillows. She said, "I'll be out of here in two days, on my feet in five and back to work in two weeks." My father and Brian had moved immediately toward the bed, but I hung back by the door. I had the flowers in my hand. They'd removed her uterus. That meant that from now on she'd calm down—no more yelling, no more crying, no more craziness. A Negro orderly came in. He brushed by me. I smelled something, a musky something, a cologne, a hair oil, something. He was going to collect her tray. He was doing his job, but as soon as he came in, there was tension in the room. My mother stopped talking. I stared at his back, at the white orderly's jacket, so much like the busboy's jacket I wore at the Ritz. The jacket slid up his arm as he lifted the tray and I saw what looked like a bracelet on his right wrist. My mother saw it, too. After he put the tray on the chest of drawers, he stood at the foot of the bed and looked down at my mother. She glared back at him.

"Hello. My name is Claude. Is there anything I can get you, Mrs. Riley?" He had an accent. He was from the Caribbean. He wasn't an American. "Can I fluff up your pillows? Can I do anything to make you more comfortable?" He was being nice. He was doing his job, but he was also being nice.

"Don't bother," my mother said.

"I can bring you some fruit juice."

"No fruit juice."

"Hawaiian Punch?"

"No Hawaiian Punch."

I handed him the flowers. "Do you want to put these in water?" I asked. His eyes were on my face just a second too long. That second was enough. He knew. It was in my eyes or my voice. Or maybe it was in my chin or my lower lip or my left eyebrow. Who knows? Who cares? I was getting sick of worrying about it. He saw right into me anyway. I had no secrets from him. He took the flowers and went down the hall looking for a pot to put them in. The scent, which had actually come from something he'd sprayed in his hair to give it a gloss, lingered in the room.

"Isn't he sweet?" my mother said, finally. "Isn't he a darling?"

"Give him a break," I said. "He's just doing his job." I was trying to control my voice. It came out very cold.

"'Oh, can I fluff up your pillows! Oh, can I get you some fruit juice!' Oh, la de da."

"That's what he's supposed to do. That's what they pay him for. He's earning his living. Leave him alone!" It was like a command.

My father said, "Don't argue with your mother, Stevie. She don't feel good!" He could command, too. He turned toward my mother. "But Stevie's right, Eileen. The guy's just doing his job."

"I want nurses. I don't want characters like him. I thought I'd have nurses."

"Eileen, if no one was willing to do hospital work, how would sick people get along? West Indians need jobs. No one else wants to do hospital work. So they do it. Why not? White men don't want to do this kind of work. Someone has to do it. Remember, it takes all kinds to make a world."

Then she said it. "Not his kind." And something snapped in me.

I'd had two shocks that day. Stiller had told me I couldn't go into the army. And Welch had destroyed McCarthy by calling him a fairy. I couldn't take any more. I wasn't about to take anymore. It came up from somewhere deep, deep inside of me. I hadn't even known I had it in me. I didn't even have a name for it till then. But it came out of my spirit.

"You're a bitch," I said to my mother. "You always were a bitch and I don't care how many operations they do on you, you'll always be a bitch." Then I knew I was going to cry. So I turned and ran down the hall. The orderly was coming back with the flowers. He said, "'Hey, man! Hey! Slow down!'" I didn't slow down. I just kept running.

I walked. I sat under a tree in a little park and cried. It felt like I cried for hours. It was like I couldn't stop. Maybe people went by and saw me. I didn't care if people saw me. I cried. I'd stop for a while, think about pain and injustice, and then cry some more. I had twenty years of crying to do. I got some of it done. Finally, though, I stopped crying. I just lay there in the grass, looking up through the limbs of the tree, through the buds. It began to get dark. The sounds in the city around me turned into night sounds. I got up and walked some more. I walked to Charles Street. I found Luanne's place. The buzzer was still broken but the street door was not locked. I went in and walked upstairs.

When I knocked at Luanne's door, I heard somebody inside say, "Someone's at the door, Luanne." Since it was a man's voice, I assumed it was Simon in there. If it was Simon, I had no right to be here. When Luanne opened the door and I saw that there were no lights on inside the apartment, I said, "I'm sorry. I didn't know Simon would be here. I should have phoned first."

"Simon's not here," she said. "Come in, Steve."

I stepped inside. The apartment was lit by a single candle resting in a saucer on one of the concrete blocks. Two men were sitting on pillows on the floor. I couldn't see their faces. It was too dark in there. Luanne took my hand and squeezed it. "What happened?" I asked. "Couldn't pay the light bill?"

"Oh, Steve," she answered.

"A romantic candlelight dinner without food? What?"

She lifted the saucer. With the candlelight flickering under her chin, I could see the bruises on her face.

"Simon's gone," she said.

We sat down together on a pillow. I held her around the waist. It was a rotten world, but you played the hand you'd been dealt. You did your best. You tried to love people. She put her head back against my shoulder. She was my friend. I'd do what I could, as a friend. I knew how to be a friend. I was good at it.

They were drinking wine. Luanne offered to get me some but I said no. She introduced me to the two men. "This is Harold Malin," she said. In the flickering candlelight, all I could see were his eyes. He said hello. "And this is his friend Morris Wetzel." Morris Wetzel didn't say anything. "Harold put on a Punch and Judy show at Rafe's nursery school this afternoon. I'm trying to get in good with the women who run the school, Miss Peabody and Miss Enfield. So I asked Harold to do it. Anyway, the kids loved it, so Miss Peabody and Miss Enfield are happy. And if Miss Peabody and Miss Enfield are happy, we're all happy, right?"

"I loved doing it," Harold Malin said.

"Rafe loved it," Luanne said. "I was watching his face. He was in seventh heaven."

"I know what you mean. I can see the children's faces through the eye hole in the curtain. When it looks as if Punch has killed the dog, Toby, the children get very quiet all of a sudden. And when Toby comes up behind Punch to bite him, they squeal and clap their hands. When the devil comes up, the young ones get frightened. You have to be careful with that."

"Miss Peabody and Miss Enfield loved it," Luanne said. "Everyone loved it. It was wonderful. Thank you, Harold. I had no idea you were so talented."

"And, as I told you before, Luanne, it takes physical strength to do puppets. I hold my arms over my head for thirty minutes during each show. And most of it is fighting, knocking my fists together. And Punch's voice is hard on the vocal cords. In the old days, the puppeteer kept a squeaker in his mouth to make that sound. And you have to have manual dexterity for the finger movements. It takes strength to do any kind of hand puppet thing, but Punch and Judy is much rougher."

He looked toward me, expecting me to say something. He wanted to include me in the conversation. He was being polite. I couldn't think of anything to say, though. He was just a voice and two eyes. You can express a lot with two eyes and a voice though. I knew. I knew about the quiet young man beside him, too. Sure, I could be brave about my homosexuality with people like Stiller, but I was confronting the real thing here, and what was I supposed to say? "I haven't seen a puppet show since I was eight years old," I said. "It was a Christmas show put on by the church. I remember liking it a lot."

"Did they use hand puppets?"

"No, the puppets were on strings. Mary and Joseph, the baby Jesus, the Three Wise Men. 'I see a star in the east!' A Christmas show."

Luanne got up to refill her wine glass. She didn't come back to sit with me. She pulled up a pillow of her own next to Harold. "Harold goes around to hospitals, giving shows for kids. I wish I could do something useful like that."

"You work with Rafe," Harold said.

"Oh, yes, Rafe. He's harder to entertain than a whole hospital full of kids. Yes, Rafe's enough for me."

I got up and walked toward the bathroom. As I passed the bedroom, I glanced in. Rafe was asleep there on the cot Luanne had bought for him, his "security blanket" in his hand. A candle in a saucer was burning down on the concrete block next to his head. There was a burning candle on the back of the toilet, too. A breeze was blowing in over the open window by the bathtub. It was nice. Sad but nice. A typical spring night in Boston. Soulful magnolias blooming behind wrought-iron fences and wistful people sitting around drinking wine and being polite together. When I went back, Harold and Morris were at the door, saying goodbye to Luanne. Harold turned to me and said, "I'm giving a show at Children's Hospital on May 13th. Why don't you attend? If you haven't seen a puppet show since you were eight years old..."

I saw Morris take a step backwards. It was as though somebody had prodded him with a sharp stick. "Hal, I'll meet you in the car," he said.

"No, I'll walk down with you. Wait."

"I'll be in Basic Training on May 13th," I said.

"Oh. The army." I noticed that he was wearing a turtleneck sweater, corduroy trousers and sandals. He was nice looking. I liked his hair.

"Yes. The army."

They left. Luanne went into the bedroom and came back with something wrapped in paper. "You said you had a birthday, so I got you this," she said. I opened it. It was a light cotton jacket. "It's too warm for peacoats," she said, smiling. "Happy birthday." I thanked her.

I did have some wine now. We sat on pillows facing each other, drinking. It felt good to have a friend like this.

"How did your day go?" she asked.

"Oh, your typical day, Luanne. Stiller told me I'd have to lie about being queer to get into the army. And I called my mother a bitch."

"How'd she react to that?"

"It can't come as news to her. She is a bitch."

"Was that your day? Anything else?"

"I cried in the park. And, let's see, I guess that's all. How about you?"

"I broke it off with Simon. Tarzan's gone back to his tree house. And to Jane."

"How do you feel about it?"

"It's life."

We talked for an hour. Rafe stumbled in, trailing his blanket, climbed into his mother's lap and cuddled there. After a while he fell asleep. "Harold Malin seemed like an interesting guy," I said. "I think he liked me. I'd like to know him better."

"Don't do it, Steve," Luanne answered. "Don't. You'll regret it for the rest of your life. Nothing is worse than that kind of life."

"What do they do that's so awful?" I asked.

"It's just terrible. It's just a terrible way to live. Please. I don't want to talk about it. Just take my word for it. I knew some men in New York. They just led terrible lives. They were always so unhappy." She thought for a minute. She laughed. Then she added, "Why does life hurt so much?"

"You don't have to be queer to be in pain," I said.

I put on the jacket before I left. "Give the peacoat to the Salvation Army," I said, at the door. "It's spring now. I don't need it any more. And I'll get a new set of clothes when I get to Fort Dix anyway. Khaki, all the rage this season."

"Oh, Steve," she said, and she kissed me goodbye. It was a light kiss on the cheek. It was nice, having a friend like that. I was happy that we were friends. I think she was happy, too. "Good luck," she whispered. And she stood in the doorway watching me as I went down the stairs.

*

Brian was in bed, under his blanket. Our room was dark. At first I thought he was asleep. Then something told me he wasn't. I got undressed and hoisted myself up into my bunk. Brian wouldn't be sleeping here much longer. He was taking that garden apartment on Dartmouth with his wife. I lay on my back and looked up at the ceiling. Finally, I said, "Was Ma mad that I called her a bitch?"

Brian answered, "Naw. She said she always knew you were crazy. She said she'd been called worse things. She said you were the one who needed a hysterectomy now. She thought it was funny."

A long time went by. Then Brian said, slowly and very clearly, "Stevie? What's wrong with you?"

I didn't answer.

He said it again. Then he said, "It's been going on for weeks. What is it?"

"I went with a woman and nothing happened. To me, nothing happened." It was becoming a formula. You laid it on Stiller, you laid it on Brian. There was no emotion connected with it any more. I'd gone beyond that.

"Oh. I see. Oh, Stevie, that's nothin'. It's happened to me."

I didn't say anything. Crazy thoughts went through my mind. Brian? Brian, also? Did it run in families? No, not Brian. That was impossible. He had Mary. "It happened to you?"

"Yeah. Last fall and winter. Mr. and Mrs. Mangan used to go to the movies, leaving Mary and myself in their house alone, y'know? They did it on purpose, I think, because... How long had Mary and I been going together, only an eternity, right? But both Mary and I were so inexperienced, it took a long time before we could enjoy intercourse every time we tried. When I'd succeed, I'd

107

think, 'What a lucky break!' And when I failed, I'd be depressed. I'd think, 'What's the matter? Is something wrong with me?'"

"Oh."

"I think it happens to everyone, Stevie. Only they don't talk about it. They're too ashamed. But it's wrong to be ashamed about it. It happens. It's normal."

"What did Mary think when you failed?"

"Oh, she didn't know what was wrong. She had no experience either, really. She used to lay there beside me, looking up. But, see, she loves me, Stevie, and I love her. That's what makes the difference. She loved me and she was willing to wait. It's such a psychological thing. Any interruption, like a phone ringing or a knock on the door, can ruin it. I was always afraid Mr. and Mrs. Mangan would come home. Like, maybe the projector broke down at the movies and there was no show. Foolish worries like that. That's why we ran off and got married. We'd had enough of the other routine. We had to make it legal, to see if that would help."

"Did it?"

"Yeah. Everything's fine now. It's the nervous system, Stevie. Men are supposed to be like rocks, but we have nerves, too. We have feelings. And, Stevie, I know what you're thinking. You're as normal as I am, believe me. You just have to find a woman you love who loves you in return. You need the right woman and a little time. I found that and you'll find it, too. Just be patient."

"And everything's O.K. for you now?"

"Oh, yeah. Sure. I don't go limp like that anymore."

He didn't say anything else. Pretty soon I could tell from his breathing that he was really asleep. I couldn't fall asleep though. I just lay there. About one A.M., I got up, dressed again, went out, and walked the empty streets of South Boston. I came home about four. I'd been the only one out there. Where were we? Where were we hiding? And why couldn't I find my real brothers? They were out there somewhere. But where?

9

Around the middle of April, I started to get up early in the morning—at five, five-thirty, six o'clock—to run at Carson Beach or City Point. I didn't plan this. It just happened. One morning I was out there walking on the sand. A minute later I was running. I didn't think, "Start running!" My body had the thought and then I did it. The body thinks too, but it does it without words. Because it does it without words, we don't have a word for what it does. Running on the track at the Y, which I'd been doing since March, was all right, but the beach was better. It wasn't only the sand and the waves and the sun coming up over the water, though that was part of it. It was that the track didn't go anywhere. I always ended up where I'd started. On the beach, I felt like I could go on forever—though the beach had its physical limits too, of course, Castle Island, Columbus Park, Columbia Point, to name only three. What I mean is, I felt like I could go on forever in my mind. The thoughts I had while running had no limits. And they were true thoughts, too. When I was running I was always sure. I always knew. All my questions had answers. I was almost always alone out there at that hour, but sometimes I'd see this old white-haired man, standing at the edge of the water, staring off toward Spain thousands of miles away, probably thinking about death, God, immortality, the kind of things an old man would think about looking out at the ocean that way at that time of day. One morning, he'd taken off his shoes and socks and waded into the water up to his ankles. I ran past the shoes and socks on the hard-packed sand. The shoes were black brogans, the kind of shoes an old man would wear. And the socks were white. He had folded the socks neatly, the way you'd fold them if you were going to lay them in a drawer. I thought it was beautiful—the way he'd carefully folded his white socks that way before he placed them next to his black shoes. The essence of the man was in the action. I used to have moments like that out there all the time. I wasn't ashamed of them either, though I knew enough not to tell anyone about them. I'd get a feeling of completeness, of unity. I'd feel connected with everything around me. The early morning light would cascade across the water and I'd see it—really experience it, in my whole body—and then it was as if lights were coming up in my soul, too. Then everything would feel right to me, as it had never felt right before. I'd come back to the three-decker, feeling joy, feeling ecstasy. And my mother would be there in the kitchen, drinking coffee, smoking her Walter Raleigh cigarette, waiting for me. "What! Have you gone 'mental?' What will the neighbors think, seeing you out there in your skivvies at six A.M.? I heard a woman talking about you in the A & P yesterday! I was so embarrassed. I thought I'd die."

"They're not skivvies. They're gym shorts."

"Well, they might as well be skivvies. Anyone looking out the window would think they were skivvies. Some morning someone's gonna call the cops on you for indecent exposure!"

"I'm getting in shape for the army."

"How come you're such a hot shot all of a sudden? What are you trying to do, get the jump on the other guys? The army will get you in shape on its own once they get you to Fort Dix. Leave it to the army. They know how to do it."

She wasn't working, which meant she was bored. She needed someone to argue with, as a way of working off nervous tension. But I always felt so good, I couldn't oblige her. All I cared about was—it was spring and I had discovered my body! I'd come into that kitchen with some clear visual image in my mind—like maybe I'd just scattered some gulls out there and as they went up into the air over the water, I'd gone with them in my mind—and she'd try to shatter it with a comment like, "What are you, some kind of Babe Didrickson Zaharias, practicing for the Marathon. Well, you missed it. It was last week. Ha!" But she never got to me.

One morning I arrived home glowing with energy and light. I said, "I wish I lived in a place where I could run on the beach every morning of the year."

"Well, forget it. This is Massachusetts, not California."

"I'd like to live in California."

"Yeah, and I'd like all the money they stole from the Brink's truck. Stevie, stop dreamin'. Grow up. Live in the real world for a change. And stop tracking that sand in here every morning. It gets all over my linoleum! I'm tired of sweeping up after you."

I'd have these thoughts, and maybe they were crazy, but what could I do? They were my thoughts and they were there. I wasn't going to pretend I didn't have them. One morning, listening to my mother complain, I heard a voice inside me say, "Is your mother beautiful in her essence?" And the answer was yes. Yes, she was. But over that "essence" there was this tough, crusty surface. I saw that surface. I saw it in my mind. It was like a piece of a pier I'd seen on the beach, all encrusted with barnacles. The image glowed there in my consciousness, like that fragment of a pier with the early morning sun shining on it. I could see every barnacle. It was beautiful. I knew I wasn't going crazy. I knew this is what it felt like to be sane! If you took all the restrictions away, removed all the stresses, were really in touch with things, this is how the world would look. I saw my mother's true self. But imagine trying to tell her about her "true self!" She'd have had me in Mass General before I could turn around. I was beginning to know something else, too. These images were sexual. They were like the visual images I'd experienced when I climaxed during masturbation. Then I knew why my people were so terrified of sex and did everything they could to throw up fences around it. Vision was religion. But it was a religion they couldn't control. They were trying to fence in the ocean with a few yards of barbed wire, and they were furious because it couldn't be done. But they kept trying.

One morning I saw an old blue denim jacket lying on some rocks below Columbia Road. I "saw" it in that special way, so it was beautiful to me. To anyone else, it would have been just a rag. But my eye fastened on it and all of a sudden there was nothing else in the world I wanted to look at right then. That jacket glowed! And it spoke to me, too, not in words—I wasn't that crazy! But it definitely said something, something about the guy who'd worn it, worn it with love apparently, worn it till it was frayed, frazzled, torn in places. The guy's essence had gone into it, into the torn pocket, into the spot of yellow paint on the right cuff. It was a work of art, I decided. So I picked it up and carried it home, intending to wash it and wear it. To me, it was like finding a king's ermine robe.

"Don't bring dirty rags in my house," my mother said.

"I intend to wash it," I said.

"Not in my machine!"

I turned, left the house, walked sixteen blocks to a public laundromat, washed it and dried it and wore it home. I told my mother, "If you touch it, if you take it, if you try to throw it away..."

"What'll you do?"

"I'll kill you."

"You're not man enough."

But she never touched the jacket. And I began to wear it every day from that point on. Oh, not the entire day. Not to work at the Ritz. But when I went to the beach to run at sunrise or during my long, lonesome walks at night. Wearing it made me happy. What did I care what people thought of me? Wasn't it a free country?

But my mother said, "Stevie, your idea of independence doesn't exist in the real world. What's going to become of you? I worry."

My father was there the morning she said this. He defended me. "Look, Eileen, we all go through this. Leave the kid alone. He can settle down later and be like everybody else. It happens too soon anyway. You want him to get a lawn mower and a cocker spaniel like that brother of yours. There's plenty of time for that."

I was never going to settle down behind a picture window with a daughter in dancing school and the *Wall Street Journal* in my den and a wife in the Junior League. I'd made a decision. Tim had told Brian, "The proudest moment of a man's life is when he finally makes a decision." Well, I'd made one. I'd decided never to be like Tim! I began to make plans for something I intended to do. One afternoon I went to an Army/Navy store and bought what I called "the indispensible item"—indispensible as far as my plan was concerned, that is. I left it with Luanne, since I couldn't keep it at home. My mother would have tried to stop me. I knew she would. And nothing was going to stop me. Soon, very soon, I'd act. Honest to God, I would. I really would.

*

One afternoon at the Ritz, an upper-class Frenchman rejected his sole Meuniere. The fish remained untouched, though the man had sniffed at it aristocratically. Dom Grasso, one of the waiters for whom I worked, approached the table, raised himself on the balls of his feet, bowed slightly and said, "Is everything satisfactory, sir?" The man waved the plate away. Dom signalled to me, a come hither motion from behind his back. I walked to the table, removed the plate and carried it to the screen which separated the dining room from the kitchen. An old Greek waiter whom I liked—he used to talk to me in a nostalgic way about his village near Corinth—was standing there. I handed him the plate and he ate the sole Meuniere. When he'd finished, I carried the plate into the kitchen.

The yelling began almost immediately, coming from the area between the dining room and the kitchen, where I'd just left the waiter. I heard it as I was about to hand the plate to one of the dishwashers. It was Frank DiPietro's day off. A guy named Angelo was taking his place as maitre d'. The waiter and Angelo came into the kitchen, Angelo screaming his head off at the waiter, the waiter looking scared. I decided to hold onto the plate, though the dishwasher had his hand out for it. As soon as the people in the kitchen heard the screaming, they all got very busy with their assigned tasks—hands began to fuss with pots and pans, a guy began to push a broom very rapidly—but no one was missing anything. Their ears were taking it all in. Everyone knew the scenario. The waiter was an old guy past his prime. He was slow and he made mistakes. He mooned around about how good life had been in the old country in the old days, which got on everyone's nerves, because everyone knew the old days had been terrible. Why else had they left? But he was a good-hearted old guy. And he was about to be fired for eating that fish, though everyone ate the delicacies the guests rejected as often as they could get away with it.

As they walked past me, I said, "I ate the fish. Leave the old guy alone." I had nothing to lose. I was going into the army soon anyway. But for the waiter... without a job, how would he live?

Angelo looked at me. Then he looked at the plate. He knew I hadn't eaten the fish, but the plate seemed to be evidence that I had. He was confused. He was basically just a stupid man with a loud voice. I raised the plate and dropped it on the floor, where it bounced a couple of times and then broke in two. The waiter was going to get fired anyway, if not today then next week or the week after, but it felt good to save him this time. Besides, I was the one who had given him the fish! Angelo was too shocked to scream. This seemed to require an additional gesture, so I ripped off my white duck jacket—not bothering to unbutton it—and threw it in his face. "I quit," I said. Then I handed him the clip-on bow tie, turned and went to the locker room.

As I was putting on the jacket Luanne had given me for a birthday present, a guy named Frank stuck his head in the door and said, "Hey, tig-aire! Tough man, you!" I was the hero of the Ritz kitchen. Big deal. All I wanted was to be outside in the sun, walking in the Public Garden, master of my own body, my own mind. Because that's all they wanted. Once they had control of your body, they could use you like a machine until you began to break down. Then they could discard you, the way they were about to discard that old waiter. And, suddenly I was free, moving past flower gardens, catching the glint of sunlight off the Swan Boat pond, responding to the faces and bodies of the young men around me, singing to myself, free as the cottonwood fluff that was everywhere in the air in Boston that afternoon. Shirts had begun to come off in the early summer heat. I got high looking at pectorals and biceps and the black body hair that asserts itself over the restraining belt buckle and curls seductively around the navel and the flat belly. Men were lying in the grass, their legs spread, giving their cocks room to breathe and grow. But I didn't know how to approach them. I didn't know what to say. I needed an opening line. I needed assurance that I wouldn't be rejected or, worse, physically assaulted. I knew that I could also be arrested and jailed. Meanwhile, skin, muscles, thighs, nipples, cocks, balls, bellybuttons, lips, tongues cried out. "Love us! Love us! Why else were we created!" I sat down in the grass next to one of the men. I said, "Hello." He gave me a blank look. Then he got up and walked away. He hadn't understood. His look had said, "Who are you? I don't know you." My heart was pounding in my chest. I felt light-headed. My throat was dry. He could have hit me. He could have held me down and hit me in the face. No one would have tried to rescue me. In the minds of the other men here, I deserved to be punished. I had violated the code. But how could something as wonderful as sex be anything but essentially good? And how could anything as fundamentally perfect as a male body be bad? And how could my affirming spirit be wrong about all this? And why couldn't I find a man with enough generosity of soul to bring me forward into full sexual life?

"You what?" my mother said when I came home that evening. "You quit!"

"Yes, I quit," I answered. The way to win with this kind of thing, I'd discovered, was to say it firmly in a calm, steady voice, while looking directly into her eyes. The person whose eyes wavered first was the loser. The person who maintained eye con-

114

tact longest was the winner. Her eyes didn't waver. Neither did mine. So we balanced there, on a pivot.

"Whenever you do something like this, other people get hurt," she told me, after she saw she couldn't outstare me. "You think you're doing it on your own, but you're not. Everything you do affects someone else. Think about me for once. I got you the job. Frank DiPietro is a friend. How do you think I'm going to feel next time I see him and he says, 'Your son is a spoiled brat!' What am I supposed to say to him, Stevie?"

"Sometimes a man has to assert himself. It's a matter of self-respect."

"Self-respect is something you earn. And you earn it by doing what you're told to do when you're told to do it. They'll teach you that in the army. If you assert yourself in the army, you'll end up in the stockade."

"I'm an adult. I have to learn to make decisions on my own!"

"Make responsible ones! Don't act like an idiot. Think about what you do before you do it! In this case, you should have thought of me! Look! It's like, books lined up on a shelf. You can't move one without disturbing all the others. You think you're acting alone, but every time you do something, it affects hundreds of other people. Think about that the next time you're tempted to step out of line."

She turned away. But her eyes had never wavered and I knew that, in her own mind, she had won. But in my mind, I had won. That meant we both had won, which meant, also, that we both had lost. Or was I wrong about that? Anyway, I knew she was right. I'd acted irresponsibly. I'd put her in a bad spot with Frank Di-Pierto. It was important to act responsibly. It was very important. It really was. I'd work at it. I would! I didn't want to hurt anybody. I just wanted to live. I just wanted to feel alive. I just wanted to step out of line, grab a man around the waist, press his body to mine and let my right hand slide caressingly down to his crotch. I wanted to cup that sweet loving handful. I wanted to squeeze it. I wanted to slide that zipper down, reach inside and warm my hand on all that heat. I wanted to bury my face in that moist, hot maleness. But my mother was right. I'd restrain myself. I'd watch it. I'd be good a little while longer.

*

I had a dream. Call it a vision. I was both asleep and awake. I was in a state which was both and neither. Brian had left for good

115

now. He had his own place with Mary. So I slept in the bottom bunk. I looked up and I saw them, standing at the foot of the bunk, spirit figures. Yes, there's no other way to describe them. They were spirits. I knew in that wordless way you can know things while in that state of consciousness that these were my ancestors. More, these were the ones who'd been queer. They stood there staring down at me. Most of them had lived out their lives in Ireland—a pale, unhappy librarian, a few embittered schoolmasters, clerks, priests, a tonsured monk or two. They'd never had the words to describe their condition or a language to express their physical and spiritual longing, though, ironically, those in this group had spent their lives transcribing or teaching languages. Their lives had been lived in an acquiescent numb silence. Their guiding spirits had whispered to them year after year, but they hadn't listened. Or they'd denied what they heard. Or there'd been no opportunities. Or they'd been timid. Or they hadn't met that other man who might have loved them and led them into life. They had died unfulfilled. Then I was aware that other ancestors were crowding in behind them and these were the ones who'd been ridiculed, reviled, beaten, jailed, burned. These had been wood cutters, sheep rustlers, rebels, roisters, village eccentrics, dancers around bonfires, mummers who led annual processions. These men had acted on their desires and been punished for their actions. Then I saw hundreds of others, all those who'd waited until middle age to marry, who'd spent their best years celibate, in pubs, throwing darts with their mates, lifelong friends with whom they did not have sex. These had done their civic and religious duty, had fathered sons and daughters, and gone down to their graves in anger and despair wondering why they had never known joy or peace or love. I saw all the alcoholics, the suicides, the cranks, the madmen, the laudanum addicts, the visionaries, the mystics. Most had lived and died alone, lonely wanderers in bogs and along seacoasts. No man had ever held them, kissed them and said, "I want you." And they had gathered at the foot of my bunk to tell me, "You are one of us. You'll live like us and die like us." And every cell in my body replied, "Oh, no I won't!" And I came to waking consciousness happy, with a smile on my face. Oh, no I won't, I thought, as I started my day. Not Little Stevie! Not me.

On the evening of May 6th, Luanne gave a party. It was a combination graduation party for her Boston University friends, many of whom were graduating, and a goodbye party for me, because the next morning at nine o'clock I was scheduled to take my pre-induction physical at the Boston Army Base. Her parties were clearinghouses for human relationships. She never bought liquor or food. She couldn't have afforded that. There wasn't even a decent place to sit down. What she provided was a space where people could come together to rearrange their lives. They came here to merge and recombine, like chemical elements in a retort. Marriages ended at her parties, love affairs began, perhaps even a few children were conceived. I'd come here after flipping a coin in the lobby of a movie theater and my life had never been the same. So that was good. There was life here, on-going life. You came here to get on with the business of living. So here we were. And what a night. Flowers were blooming all over the Back Bay in a soft erotic haze. And because so many people were being released from the cocoon of formal education, everybody was in a frenzy to recombine. Oh, it wasn't evident at first, while people were still sober, but about eleven o'clock it got wild.

Harold Malin was there with his sad-faced friend Morris. Morris didn't hang around long. One minute he was there, the next minute he was gone. This didn't seem to bother Harold any, though they'd arrived together. He sat down on a concrete block and began to play his guitar. He sang folk songs—"Greensleeves," "The Joys of Love," songs like that. People weren't really interested in this. They were polite for a while, but then they wandered off. Maybe he wasn't all that good. Maybe he manipulated puppets more effectively than he sang. Or maybe these were just the usual rude, insensitive people Luanne had stocked earlier parties with. Because I was convinced he had something—magnetism, presence, charm. Also, he was good-looking, with those large eyes and that nice smile. And I liked his hair, which was a rich chestnut brown. When Luanne sang later—"I've been in love before, you'll see! Oh, darling, what a bore I'd be!"—her guests ignored her. I drew her aside and told her I thought they were terrible.

"Oh, yes. But after tonight I'll never see any of them again anyway. I don't need them anymore. My ex-husband's coming to Boston tomorrow. He got a gig at Birdland."

"A gig?"

"A job. He's a musician. Plays the sax. You didn't know. He's a jazz musician. Anyway, he'll be staying with me. He's through with the bitch in New York. It's the long-term commitments that count—marriage, a child. Lovers come and go, mostly go. But some relationships are forever."

I laughed, remembering something. "You know, Luanne, this seems like it happened a hundred years ago. But once in the Tip Top, Ralph said he heard that you stole five hundred bucks out of your husband's wallet and ran off to New York."

"Honey, if I'd ever been lucky enough to find a husband who had five hundred bucks in his wallet, why would I ever have left him and gone to New York? Would I have dumped a meal ticket like that? Have you ever known anyone who kept that amount of money in a wallet?"

I had to admit I hadn't. "Well, Ralph told me that."

"It was a checking account. The money was half mine. And it was two hundred dollars. And it wasn't my husband. And if I hadn't done it, I'd never have left Saint Louis and I wouldn't be standing here now talking to you!"

And we'd never have gone to bed together and at this moment I'd be...where? "Do you believe in fate?" I asked.

"I believe in love," she answered. Then she laughed. "Love and marriage. They go together. Like a horse and carriage."

Well, maybe so, but there were at least half a dozen people here so heavily, so unhappily into marriage, they were ready to shed their spouses at the drop of a bra strap. When you're tied down, it's natural to want to be free. When you're free, you wake at three A.M. and think about love and marriage. That was just human nature. Only in the transitional phase from one condition to another could you be happy, as Luanne was now.

There was a note thumbtacked to the bedroom door: CHILD SLEEPING. DO NOT DISTURB. Luanne said, "Rafe was conceived at a party, born after a party and he's slept through hundreds of parties since then. But tomorrow his daddy's going to be here and he was so excited when I told him. Isn't life grand?"

Later I asked her where she'd put the "indispensible item" I'd asked her to keep for me. She opened the broom closet next to the sink. It was in there, on the floor. "We all have our dreams, Stevie," she said. "But yours is so wild, I just can't believe you'll actually do it."

"Oh, I'll do it. I'm definitely going to do it."

"Well, you probably will. And I'll get back with Martin again. And we'll all live happily ever after in la-la land!"

Harold, who was graduating, had brought six bottles of champagne. He said his father, who owned a restaurant in Millbrae, California, had sent a case as a graduation present. California champagne. Imagine having a father who'd do a great

118

thing like that! He said, "I always write the date on the cork when it's a memorable occasion like a graduation." There were six corks. He popped them all. Everyone wanted corks, so he threw them up in the air. I caught one. A ball point pen went around and I wrote the date on mine: May 6, 1954. Then I put the cork in my pocket. I watched him going around filling up Dixie cups. There were never enough glasses at Luanne's. Most people drank beer from bottles. He was wearing a Boston University sweatshirt, red and white, the school colors, gray corduroy trousers and sneakers. Under the clothing, he had a neat, compact, sexy little body. There was just the right amount of magic in it, just the right amount of controlled energy. I thought, "There's no way it could ever be him!" He was just too good! But I was going to give it a try. After tomorrow, unless I told the truth on that form, I'd be in the army and…that would be that. I'd be under continual observation. I wouldn't be able to do anything.

After everyone had had champagne, he sat down on a pillow across the room. No one was sitting with him, so I went over and sat down on the floor beside him. "Tell me about your father's restaurant," I said. It seemed like a pretty good opening line. But any line would have been a good one. He was a friendly guy. There was nothing snooty about him.

He looked at me. I could tell he liked me. He liked everything. You could see that. It just showed. "There's a deck. It looks out on a golf course," he said. "The golf course used to be a prune orchard."

"Thanks for the champagne." I took another sip of it. "It was nice of you to bring it."

"You came in the other night, the night we had candles because of Luanne's bruises. When you walked in, I thought you were a dyke." He laughed. I didn't know what to say, so I didn't say anything. I figured I'd listen and learn. "It was the peacoat and the boots. Then, after I heard your voice, I realized you were a man. Of course it was dark. I thought Luanne had finally figured herself out and decided she wanted a woman after all. Then you turned out to be a man."

"Luanne has terrible luck with men."

"She wants it that way," he said.

"Her husband's coming back."

"Yes, for a weekend. Or perhaps a week. Have you met him?"

"No."

He didn't say anything else about Luanne or her husband. "Being in Boston for four years has been interesting. But I'm ready to go back to California. I'm eager to start working."

"What do you do?"

"I'll be teaching children at a country day school near Los Gatos. I like working with children. What do you do?" He talked with a flat precision that made my Boston accent jar on my ears.

"I'm going into the army. I take my physical examination at the army base tomorrow." I tried to talk more like him. It didn't sound right. Now I was self-conscious. I stopped talking. He stopped talking, too. He excused himself and went across the room to talk to someone else. I'd never really been aware of it before, but when I talked I sounded funny. That diminished me in my own eyes. Also, he must be rich, if his father owned a restaurant that looked out on a golf course and could afford to send a case of champagne like that. And he was Jewish, which made him very different from working class Irish South Boston Stevie! Christ, I wasn't going to get to first base with this guy. But I decided to keep trying. After all, what did I have to lose? So I sat there trying to figure out some kind of strategy. I couldn't come up with any though. I just hit a blank wall. Maybe I should just give up, I thought. I couldn't decide. I'd flip a coin and let it depend on the toss. But I didn't have a coin. The only thing I had in my pocket was a champagne cork with the date on it.

Around midnight, someone turned off the lights. All of a sudden people were hugging and kissing all around me. They weren't "Happy Graduation" kisses either. They were hot and heavy and sexual. It was that kind of night. It was in the air—a potent sexual electricity. At the moment the apartment went dark, I was in the kitchenette leaning against the sink. Harold was beside me. People were packed together like beans in a jar. You couldn't move. The noise, the smoke, the confusion, and then the sudden darkness. It was really something. To take it you had to be drunk, and I wasn't drunk, just a little silly on the champagne. I heard Hal singing softly to himself, "Graduation's almost here, my love! Teach me, tonight." I looked at his face. I'd never seen his face in daylight. Think of that! And I never would unless I acted now. "Do you want to get out of here, Harold? Go for coffee or something?"

"There's a coffee shop in the basement of this building," he said.

"Yes," I answered, though I knew it would be closed. "Let's go there."

120

I found my denim jacket and we left the apartment. I saw Luanne in the hall and she saw me, but I didn't say goodbye. There were too many people crowded in around her. I heard her yell, "Honey, wait!" But it was too late. I was already heading down the stairs. I caught up with Harold partway down. "This party can only end in one way," he said. "With police sirens. Then everyone will be arrested. I think we're getting out just in time." We stepped over a man and a woman who were lying side by side, kissing, on the landing. The woman's dress was up over her thighs. The man had a hard-on. You could see it sticking up under his trousers. "Luanne gives these incredible parties. No one's ever the same afterwards."

"Yes," I said. "I've noticed that, too."

The coffee shop was closed, naturally. I figured he had known it would be closed, too, and had just wanted to get out of all that madness upstairs. But here we were, anyway, just Harold and Steve! He leaned against the railing and said, "There's a White Tower in Kenmore Square. It's open all night. Would you like to go there?"

"That sounds good to me," I said.

We walked toward his car along Charles Street. "By the way, Steve, no one calls me 'Harold' except Luanne. Luanne and I took a class together at Boston University. The professor used to hand around a class list every day so that we could sign in for attendance. I was down as 'Harold Malin.' She saw that name on the sheet every day. That's why she calls me 'Harold.' But I want you to call me 'Hal.' Everyone calls me 'Hal' except Morris. Morris calls me 'Binky.'"

"Binky?" What would it feel like to call him "Binky?" I decided I didn't want to. If Morris called him "Binky," I definitely wanted to call him something else. "Your friend Morris left the party early," I said.

"Morris is a free agent. He can come and go as he pleases."

"He seems so sad. Doesn't he ever smile?"

"He's from New Jersey. People seldom smile in New Jersey."

There were questions I wanted to ask about his relationship with Morris, really basic ones, like, "Do you sleep in the same bed?" But I didn't have the guts. I also didn't have the language. The word "friend" didn't quite cover the relationship. But no other word was available to me at that moment.

121

We stopped next to a sharp little red MG glistening with sheets of the powerful moisture that was in the air that night. This exotic red toy was his car! Sitting there under the streetlamp, it glowed with a fiery incandescent light. The shadows of the new leaves on the trees up above flickered and flashed all over the scarlet gloss. It said, unmistakably, "rich," "privileged," "connections," "education," "social class." It said, "Jewish." It said, "Rich Jew." It said, "Other!" All the mean little hatreds, the resentments, the spite I'd been brought up with in South Boston flashed into sudden surprised life in my cells. Hate niggers, hate kikes, hate...! "This is the greatest car I have ever seen, Hal! I'm almost afraid to get into it."

"If you don't get into it, we can't get coffee."

I ran a finger over the moisture that lay so erotically over the red paint. I looked down into the seat where I'd be sitting. The top was down and the tree up above had dropped winged seeds onto the leather. I leaned in and picked up a seed. He went around to the driver's side and got in. God, he had nice hair! Such a nice color. Suddenly I had a thought. He was an almost total stranger. And he was completely different from me in every possible way. We had absolutely nothing in common. If we hadn't both been queer, we could never have met. We certainly wouldn't have been here, now, together like this. Also, it was one thing to leave a party with a stranger. It was something else to enter into his life and that's what I'd be doing if I got into the car. We were just going for coffee at a White Tower. But I knew better. If it ends with coffee, I told myself, I will jump off the Northern Avenue Bridge. He leaned over and opened the door on my side. His hair slid forward over his forehead. God! How beautiful. I got in. We started off up the avenue. He was still singing to himself. "One thing isn't very clear, my love. Should the teacher act so queer my love. Graduation's almost here, my love. Teach me tonight." I was sucking on the seed.

"The car was my older sister's," Hal said, as we moved in traffic up Commonwealth Avenue. "She got married and didn't want it anymore, so she gave it to me."

"You mean, she sold it to you."

"No, she gave it to me. She wanted a bigger car. This one wasn't right for her anymore. I wish I had a larger car. Driving two thousand miles with Morris in this one... Oh, Morris is driving back with me to California. I'd never set out in this without someone to help with the driving. And what if it broke down in Utah or Nevada?"

"What's it like out there? I've never been out of Boston."

"What do you think it's like?"

"Exciting. Wild. Awesome. Terrific."

"Well, it is if you want it to be. Or it can be... Driving through it can be difficult. When you get through Iowa and into Nebraska, the roads get bad. The desert is beautiful. But... difficult driving."

"I read that you have to drive through the desert at night. Because of the heat."

"Well, no. That's not true."

The moist air was blowing over my body. I wanted to be naked in it. I wanted to be naked with the dew on my skin, standing up in this seat shouting joyously to the people in the cars around us. We passed the Beaconsfield Hotel with its Governor Bradford Room. That brought me back to reality. Hal's father actually owned a restaurant. My people worked in them. What would the Governor Bradford Room mean to Hal? He'd go there to be waited on, to eat, to entertain friends. Did he leave large tips? Is everything satisfactory, Mr. Malin? Broiled mackerel with mint? Shad roe? Veal cutlet, Vienna style? Pears in wine?

He offered me a cigarette. "No, thanks," I said. "I don't smoke. Bad for the lungs. I'm a runner. I watch my body."

"I notice you don't drink much either."

"Right. I don't drink much."

"What do you do?"

"I... I do everything but smoke and drink," I answered, knowing, as I said it, that I was lying and would have to pay for this later. But this was ridiculous! I wasn't a high school girl on a prom date. I was a man. I'd do anything he wanted to do. I'd do what came naturally. I'd just let it happen. Then I'd know. At least I'd know. I'd have done it with a man. I'd have had that experience. And no army could ever take that away from me.

But he said, "We're going for coffee at the White Tower, that's all." It was as if he could read my thoughts. I was immediately disappointed. I was also hurt. I said, "Why?" There was a big emptiness in me now. I was being rejected. He didn't want me. I wasn't going to have this experience after all. It hurt. I wasn't going to have him! I kind of hated him at that moment. I wanted to get out and walk home.

"I'm not going to bring you out," he answered. "I've been there. You'd wake up in the morning hating me. It's not worth it. Sorry."

The White Tower was mobbed. We finally got to sit down at a metal table pushed up against the window. The waitress slammed down two cups of coffee in thick white mugs. The mugs rang on the metal. Mine had a lipstick stain on the rim. I turned that side away. I'd drink out of the other side.

My problem was, I didn't have the language. How could I manage without it? "What do you mean 'bring me out?'" I asked. I said it sort of low. I was so hurt. I could hardly control my voice. He couldn't hear me. The place was very noisy. I raised my voice. "I don't know what you mean. You say you won't 'bring me out!' Why? What are you talking about?"

He shook his head. I looked at him. He wasn't the beautiful person I'd met at the party. He was someone totally "other." No, he was still beautiful. I was just angry and hurt. No, he was a stranger. I was sitting with a total stranger. "Have you ever had sex with a man?" this total stranger asked me. "The first time I saw you, I thought you were a lesbian. Then I thought you were a straight man. Then I talked to Luanne about you and she said you were a straight man who thought he was gay. She said you had sex with her and then decided you liked guys. I don't know what you are. You're different. I'm afraid of you. I mean, I'm afraid to have sex with you. I don't know where you're coming from. What are you anyway?"

The White Tower was not the right place to have this conversation. Probably no place was the right place. "I... I know I'm queer."

"You don't act it. You don't have any of the mannerisms. And don't say 'queer.'"

This was no better than being with Stiller! You can't know it in your mind because your thoughts change. You can't know it in your body because how can your liver and heart know anything? So how do you know? I just know! That's not good enough. Sorry! And Stevie gets the boot. "How do you know you are?" I asked.

"I have sex."

"Well, I want to have sex, too!"

"But then, afterwards, you'll hate me for bringing you out. It's not that simple. I don't want to be the one who brings you out. I don't want all that grief. I don't need it. It's not worth it."

"You're telling me I'm not worth it." I could get up and leave. I could go to the subway stop in Kenmore Square. I could go back to South Boston... No. It was after midnight! The cars had stopped running. It wasn't fate that controlled my life. It was the fucking MTA! "I'm sorry. I have to tell myself I am worth it. If I'm going to live with myself, I have to insist on that. So don't tell me I'm not worth it. I am!" As soon as I could see by the expression on his face that he would have no reply to this, I said, "I am worth it!"

The waitress came back. She was a poor broken-down working-class woman with pain written all over her face. She was like my mother. She was my kind of people. No, Hal told her. We weren't going to eat. We just wanted coffee. Well, there were a lot of people waiting who did want to eat. Could we sit at the counter? I certainly did not want to continue this conversation at the counter. I heard Hal say to her, "We have a right to sit here. We intend to sit here. We're not going to the counter. Thank you." Christ, he thought he was at the Ritz! She said it was a rule. If it was crowded, you had to have coffee at the counter. Or you had to order a hamburger. "Do you want a hamburger?" he asked me. I said no. "Then I guess we ought to get out of here," he said. I agreed. I left a dollar tip. Poor waitress! What chance had she ever had in life? Going out, we had to fight our way through college kids in prom clothes fighting to get in. I heard one of these Harvard types say, "The White Tower! Slumming!" But I thought, "The White Tower. My life!"

We drove around the city. The car radio played late night music. Music for Lovers. "Isn't it romantic? Just to be young on a night such as this? Da da da!" Romantic? It should have been. It wasn't. I realized I hated this city. I hated its repressions, its oppressions, its denials, its incredible cruelty. I hated what it did to people. I hated its selfishness, its lack of generosity, its blindness. I had hated what I saw it doing to outcasts like me and I had dreamed that outcasts would be more loving and generous to each other. I'd been wrong. But then, why should they be? We parked somewhere. There was a big park down below. Boston was a city of parks. It was supposed to be a big deal. Urban planning, green spaces. It meant the city fathers cared. Anyway, I sat there looking out at the trees. There sure were a lot of trees. I had no idea where we were. Hal lit a cigarette. We sat there in silence for a long time. The music was nice though. Frank Sinatra. He knew about lovers. He'd fucked Ava Gardner. That's what it was all about—fucking Ava Gardner.

Hal finished his cigarette. Then he said, "What do you see?"

See? "Uh. What do you mean?"

"Just tell me what you see."

"I see the windshield. I see the windshield wipers. I see your hand on the steering wheel. I see some trees out there. A street light. No, two street lights. Apartment houses over there, in the distance. What?"

"People? Do you see people?"

I looked. "I see someone walking a dog over there. There's someone on that little bridge."

"They're *in the life.*"

"How do you know that? C'mon, Hal. Give me a break."

"There are a hundred men down there in the bushes and they're all having sex. If you want to find out what it's all about, go down there. Pick one. Have sex. You don't have to do anything. Tell him you're trade. That means you don't go down. Let him go down on you. He'll bring you out."

"I'd rather stay here."

"Why?"

"Oh, because a bird in the hand is worth two in the bush." Might as well make a joke of it.

"No, sometimes two in the bushes is worth more. Besides, your hand's not on my bird. And it's not in my bush either." He laughed.

I leaned over toward him. He stopped laughing. I kissed him. It was really nice and it went on for a long time. I felt the shock in his body. Then that went away. He relaxed. I ran the tip of my tongue along his lower lip. I cupped the back of his head, getting my fingers into all that lovely hair. I touched the back of his neck as gently and lovingly as I had ever touched anything in my life. I could smell and taste the tobacco, but that was part of him. Anything that was part of him was fine and I wanted to absorb it through my senses. I wanted to breathe him in, all of him. His eyes closed. I brushed my lips against his eyelids, his eyelashes. I ran my lips along his cheekbones, his cheeks, really just barely breathing on his skin. I reached down into that Boston University sweatshirt and touched the warm skin on his chest with the tips of my fingers. I touched his nipples. My hand moved around until it was between his chest and his upper arm. I could feel his heart beating. I felt the body heat, the suggestion of sweat, the essences being distilled at that moment by his body. I allowed every good, gentle, loving thing inside myself to flow out of me and into him. And suddenly I knew how I knew. It just came to me. Or rather, a voice inside me that said it to me. "You don't know it in your body. You don't know it in your mind. You..."

I drew away. His eyes opened very slowly. It was so beautiful, just to see them open that way. "I know how I know," I whispered.

He didn't say anything. But his whole face seemed to be saying, "How?"

"But if you're not going to take me with you," I said, "Please take me home to South Boston. Or take me to a pay phone. I should call my parents to tell them where I am."

"You can phone them from my place," he said. Then he turned the key in the ignition. He put the car in gear. And we moved forward.

We went to his apartment. I hoped he wouldn't turn on the lights. He didn't. I hoped he wouldn't take off his clothes right away. I just wanted to love him for a while through his clothing, around his clothing, half in and half out of his clothing. He didn't take off his clothes right away. We lay on the bed for a long time, kissing, touching, exploring. We just flowed together. Most of the stuff I'd been told about making love was crap, I realized, straight crap from straight movies. But flowing together, in a world you were creating together with your lips and fingers, that part was true. So they got that part right. Maybe they heard it from a gay man and put it in the movies, who knows? Or was that ever really in the movies? Maybe not. Maybe we made it true by doing it. And music? They got that right. We had music. Hal put on the *Preludes* of Claude Debussy. Not that we really needed music. But it was nice. And the nicest thing was, the niceness went on for a long, long time. We were in no hurry. In fact, I remember Hal saying, "We'll make it last." I hoped I wouldn't say or do anything that would ruin it. I hoped he wouldn't. I didn't. He didn't. It just flowed. We just flowed with it. No problems. And we didn't need to say much. We were communicating wordlessly and it was beautiful. Like, without words, but getting it across perfectly, "I wonder what it would feel like if I just, lovingly, gently, caressingly placed my lips against your bellybutton this way." And then the gentle shock and the waves, waves spreading out over his body like light over the ocean on the first day of creation. And Hal, without words, "I would like to ease you gently up toward my face so that I can kiss you. This is because I like you. I care for you. And this is what I want to do at this moment." Umm. "And I want to introduce the tip of my tongue to the intricate little curliques of your right ear and I want my tongue to explore that area of your body. And I want to breathe my Self into you. And I want to explore the mysteries in your body, the whole history of your body." "And I want to smell the hair that drops across your forehead that way. I want to take all of that rich human perfume into myself. I want to take you into myself. I want you." "You have me." "We have each other."

Then we were naked and that was nice, too. Not nicer. It was all nice. You reach a certain plane of niceness, you don't make distinctions. I loved his body. I loved loving his body. I loved exploring his body with my lips, fingers and tongue. He said, "I've always had a thing for redheads. Your skin's..." "What?" "Different. Exotic." "I like that. I like the way you said that. I'm different. I'm unique. I think that's great!" And it was. Why be like anyone else? Why not be special! And when we were naked, I slid my mouth down his body from his neck to his thighs, going very slowly, exploring every inch of it, and came up sharply against his erect cock.

This was a test. "If you suck cock, you're queer for life!" Dozens of schoolyard louts and bullies had drilled that into my terrorized brain cells. "A man that puts his mouth on another man's cock, he ain't worth shit. He'll do anything after that. It's the lowest thing a man can do." "Suck my dick, faggot! Ha ha!" "O'Bannion owes for blows!" "Beat him up after school. Fuckin' faggot!" They were all there in the eternal brutal schoolyard of my consciousness, every one of them. They were ready to beat me down with fists, sticks, baseball bats. They were ready to kick me in the groin. They were gathering to destroy me. I said to myself, "Do you want to do this?" The answer was, "Yeah! I want to do this!" I want to do this and I want to do it one better. I don't want to just suck it. I want to venerate it, to worship it, to deify it! With everything in me then, I kissed it, right on the tip, defying all of them, casting them back into the pit they'd all crawled out of! Then I took it in my mouth and sucked it. And it tasted good! So good!

I climaxed first. It happened while I was lying against him, partly on him. I was carried off into a far place in my mind, as though on wings. I went over fields, oceans, mountains. I went up into the sky. His fingers were very gently massaging my neck. I kissed him kind of desperately as I spun off into space passing planets and suns. I held on real tight. I heard him say, "That's wonderful. Oh. Yes. Just hold me like that. That's great!" He climaxed later, masturbating. Ooh! It was so exciting to watch him doing that. I had wondered. "How do men do it?" Well, they bopped! Or they did variations on bopping. But mostly it was what? An ecstatic, delirious ditty bop! Yeah. A ditty bop with love! Wow.

I was all tangled up in his arms and legs and we were falling asleep in the sheets and the blanket. Right on the edge of sleep, I whispered, "You want to know how I know I'm like you?"

There was a softness in his voice, because he was so close to sleep. He said, "How?"

And I answered, "I know it in my soul."

10

I woke up. In a bed in an apartment on Huntington Avenue in Boston, Massachusetts, next to a man named Hal Malin. I knew what time it was, too—five A.M.—because there was a clock on the table next to the bed. And I knew, also, that it was May 7, 1954, and that at nine A.M. I would enter the army base for my physical exam. I not only knew where I was, I knew it was the right place for me to be at that time in my life and I felt at home there. I could hear Hal breathing, the most human sound in the world, someone breathing peacefully in his sleep. He was turned away from me. I leaned over and kissed him on a nice warm spot below his left shoulder. I left my lips there for a long time. It felt good to do that. By snuggling down a little, I could place my chest and stomach against his back, my cock along the crack of his ass. I could feel the heat and energy in that crack radiating through my cock. I could ride with him very gently in his rhythmical breathing. I could breathe in harmony with him. I was happier at that moment than I'd been at any time since my fifteenth year. But I had to get up. I had to pee.

The apartment was really just one large room with tall windows that looked out on the avenue. The shades were down. When this building had been a private home, before it had been divided up into apartments, this room had been the front parlor. Hal had painted the walls white. He had varnished the floor. He'd made the place his own, an expression of his personality. Everything in the place belonged there—the workbench in the corner where he made his puppets, the painting over the workbench of a juggler balancing four balls, the wicker chairs, the plants. Everything had a purpose. And the position of everything had been considered. I'd never been in a place where everything had been arranged in a certain way just because it looked good that way. He'd told me this last night. "The reason is, to delight the eye, to appeal to the senses in some way." And yet… What was wrong? I felt a tension in my body. I didn't belong here after all. I was just kidding myself about that. I'd spent only a few hours here. It had about as much to do with me as a park bench. In an hour or two I'd be gone and it would be as though I'd never been here. I stood in front of a watercolor he'd hung on the wall near the bathroom door. It showed a young man in a desert landscape. The man had a knapsack over his shoulders. There were words written under the figure: THREE HOURS AGO THE PACIFIC SEEMED CLOSE NOW IT DISAPPEARED. I could see myself reflected in the glass—Steve Riley, naked in a strange room, with an erect cock, needing to pee. "Morning, Steve," I whispered, putting my lips close to the glass.

As I stood over the toilet peeing, I listened to the traffic on the avenue. There wasn't much of it at this hour, but it was out there. We weren't far from the Back Bay Fens, the Museum of Fine Arts, the Isabella Stewart Gardner Museum, Symphony Hall, the YMCA where I ran and swam. I'd seen all this last night as we drove up the avenue, monumental buildings in a hazy blue light, an imperial street, a street designed for parades, for state occasions, for senators, soldiers, visiting dignitaries. The whole avenue proclaimed the power of the Commonwealth of Massachusetts. But Hal had found this house and moved in and transformed part of it and made it human, made it his. I looked through the window into the garden. Lilacs were blooming there in a purple mist. It looked like rain. Yes, definitely. It would rain some time today. On the gingerbread porch out there, I saw Keith bedded down on some grass in his cardboard box. Keith was Hal's pet duck. I'd said, before we undressed, "Hal, I don't think I can do it with a duck on the bed." So he'd carried it out on the porch. I'd had sex with a man who had a pet duck named "Keith." More, Hal had told me, "I call him Keith because that's the name I wanted to be called as a little boy." Proclaim that in the streets of South Boston. Publish that on your playground walls. And be sure to include, "I sucked his cock!" This bravado should have made me feel good. Instead, the tension in my body just kept increasing.

I thought I heard someone moving around in the apartment upstairs. Morris lived up there. He'd come into the house last night. I'd heard someone fumbling at the front door and Hal had said, "It's Morris. Don't worry. He'll go upstairs to his own apartment." And he had. He'd stumbled on the stairs. He was a little drunk. "He's in love with a violinist who plays with the symphony," Hal had explained. "It is going very, very badly. And Morris is very upset." I was involved with men who fell in love with violinists! I looked at the mirror over the sink. I had never seen a mirror like this in my life. The frame was in the shape of a shield. It had a lion's head at the bottom, but instead of whiskers the lion had leaves, leaves flowing out of its flaring nostrils. There was a cupid's face carved into the top of the thing and some other things on it—roses, oak leaves, some grapes. And it had been gilded. "You can pick up really good things at a schlock shop," he'd said. "Schlock" meant junk. I was learning Yiddish words. What was this, a gay version of Abie's Irish Rose? What if I went home and used Yiddish words in front of my father! Hal wasn't at ease with his Jewishness either. Even I could tell that. He used Yiddish words as a way of denying his insecurity, but I knew it was there. I'd figured out that he talked with such precision because he was afraid of "sounding Jewish." There was nothing really wrong with being Jewish, I felt. But I was Irish-Catholic, and there was everything in the world wrong with that. We were bigoted, hateful, anti-intellectual, conservative, stupid, brutal. We hated everybody, every race, every religion, every social group. We even hated ourselves. And we weren't even ashamed of it. We proclaimed it! Look at Joe McCarthy! We were proud of our bullying, pushy viciousness. How had we gotten that way? I didn't know. But part of it was in me and I hated it. Why couldn't I kick this thing?

I went back into the room and looked for the record Hal had played last night. I wanted to write down the name of a particular Prelude I'd really liked. He'd told me the name, but I'd forgotten it. It was French. Oh, yeah. Here it is. *La fille aux cheveux de lin...*

Hal's eyes opened. He saw me writing. He said, "What are you doing over there?"

"I'm educating myself."

"Come over here. Let me educate you, all right?"

I went over and got under the sheet with him.

"You know, Voltaire would say you're still not queer. You're good, but once is not enough. 'Once a scientist. Twice a sodomite.' You're still a scientist."

"Did Voltaire say that?"

"Yes. Voltaire said it."

I turned in his arms so that my whole body was pressed against his. I let my cock slide between his thighs. "Well, let's knock off a piece for this guy Voltaire," I said.

It was meant to be funny, but it didn't come out that way. He asked me what was wrong. I said there was nothing wrong, but he knew better. He said this is what he'd been afraid of. He must have had a terrible experience in the past bringing someone out. I didn't want to even ask him about it. "It's O.K.," I said. "Don't worry. Nothing's wrong."

He wasn't buying it. He said I should talk it out, get it out in the open. I mentioned the duck. I mentioned the mirror. I even said I felt funny about the duck's name. Hal lit a cigarette. I'd moved away from him now. I was lying beside him, my head resting on the pillow.

"The duck was given to me by the children at Mercy Hospital for an Easter present after a puppet show. It was the appropriate gift. Of course, it was more of a duckling then, just a ball of yellow fluff. Most Easter presents die. Chicks, rabbits—they get sick and die. I kept the duck alive. Before I go to California, I'll give it to my friend Terry, who has a farm in Walpole. Keith will never be a farm duck. He's imprinted to waddle around after human beings. But Terry will keep it in his kitchen or on his back porch. I admit, calling it 'Keith' is an affectation, but I'm full of affectations. That's the way I am."

I felt like a fool. I was a fool! But what could I do? I had to be honest. I had no choice, did I? And he had insisted that I tell him.

"What you're doing is, you're projecting your bad feelings onto a duck. It's not the duck. It has nothing to do with the duck. As for the mirror, I bought it in Southern Germany when I was over there with the army. There's a rococo church there called 'Wieskirche.' It's full of objects similar to that mirror. It is almost unimaginably loaded up with objects like that. Every square inch of the church had something like that in it. It's ecstasy in wood. There's no other way to describe it. The church was created by peasants and local craftsmen. It's an expression of their lives, of their joy in existence. It's a prosperous farming area, near mountains and lakes. None of the men who carved the objects think of themselves as faggots, as far as I know. The concept is so new, isn't it? I mean, the idea that if an object is beautiful only a faggot would associate himself with it. Or a faggot would have had to create it because real men don't know or care anything about beautiful objects. Imagine telling a craftsman in Nuremberg, as he's sitting in front of his house smoking his pipe and drinking his beer, with five sons and daughters at his feet, that he's a faggot because he carved a beautiful rococo object out of oak."

I wished he'd look at me. But he wouldn't. He just kept smoking, staring straight ahead of him. It wasn't my fault I'd been brought up among frightened, angry people who hated life. It wasn't my fault that it got passed on to me. I hadn't asked to be brought up among people who hated beautiful things. It wasn't my fault I'd heard nothing all my life except, "Hate faggots!" And I was a faggot myself, wasn't I? And I had this awful thing inside me, this class thing. It was in the air I breathed. Was that my fault?

"They have puppet theaters in Germany," he went on. "It's an important thing there. In Munich there are two puppet theaters, one for hand puppets, one for marionettes. They do the plays of Shakespeare. Imagine! I saw *A Midsummer Night's Dream* there. I went to the Kirst Kinder market, the Christmas toy fair in Nurnberg. Play isn't just for children there and toys aren't sissy items, something you have to pack away at the age of twelve and feel ashamed of. I make puppets. They're basically just dolls. I'm not ashamed that I make dolls. I do good things with them. See them over there? On the work table? Right now I have a concept in my mind about *Through the Looking Glass*. Have you read the Alice books? No. All right. But anyway, Steve, there's a famous illustration showing Alice on a mantle above a fireplace. She's half in and half out of the mirror. I've been wondering how to create that mirror effect in a puppet theater. I'd use some kind of shiny gauze—strips of it hanging down perhaps—and she could pass through it. It could be quite striking. Children are excited by effects like that. It's magic to them. They're always passing in and out of different worlds anyway, the child's world, the adult worlds of their parents and teachers. But they respond to the technical problems, too. What they really want to know after the show is, 'How did you do that?'"

Hal did look at me now and I wished he hadn't.

"I was a soldier. The Germans only saw my uniform. They're trained to respect uniforms. They didn't see the Jew, not right away anyway. And they didn't see the faggot. Not at all. They never saw me! I mean, the real me. I saw their death camps there though. They're turning them into museums. They're preserving them as monuments."

He stubbed out his cigarette in an ashtray, got up and went to the bathroom. When he came back, he had a robe on. He didn't get into bed again.

"You'll be all right, Steve. You're a very loving and sweet person. That's a wonderful thing, to have those qualities. You are a very fortunate person. I'm going down to the kitchen now to make breakfast for the three of us—you, me, Morris. It will be your pre-induction physical breakfast. About eight or thereabouts I'll drive you over to the army base. Once that ordeal is over for you, I want you to phone me. We'll meet for lunch. I'll treat you to lunch."

"I thought you were going to ask me to leave."

"Why did you think that?"

"Because I'm a fool," I answered.

6:45 A.M. At breakfast, in the kitchen in the basement, I talked to Morris about California. Hal had said they were leaving on the 27th. My conversation with Morris went this way.

I said, "Sunshine."

He said, "It rains there all the time."

I said, "But it's warm there."

He said, "San Francisco never warms up."

I said, "But a person could swim in the ocean in California all year long."

He said, "The water's too cold. No one swims."

I said, "There are deserts in California."

He snapped, "Why don't you look at a map!"

Then he walked out, went upstairs, entered his apartment and slammed the door behind him. The crash fractured the air.

Hal was looking at me with an amused expression on his face. "He's always at his worst in the morning," he said. "He's a little hung over, too."

"He's such a pain in the ass! Hal, how do you stand it?"

"He is a bit hard to take sometimes."

"A bit!"

"A lot," Hal admitted.

This Morris was the most obnoxious son of a bitch I'd ever met, and yet Hal seemed to see something worthwhile in him. But what? How had they met and what held them together? Where could I cut in on a relationship like this one in an attempt to understand it? Forget Morris! Where could I cut in on Hal's life in an attempt to understand him? He'd told me he was twenty-four. Where was I supposed to begin? Birth? The age of five? Puberty?

135

Adolescence? That would be interesting. What kind of sex did he have? I'd like to know about that! And when did he know about himself? But there was nothing to hold onto! I had a few subjective impressions, some visual images—mostly of glass walls, sheer surfaces I could never climb—but what were they worth? I suspected Hal was essentially selfish, arrogant, even ruthless about his "craft" and "the play element," as he called it, in his life. No one was ever going to come between him and his "vocation," and yet what was that "vocation" worth? He made dolls and manipulated them from behind a curtain in order to amuse children. That's all.

The coffee was strong and rich and good. I mentioned how good it was. "I go to an Italian grocery store in the North End and have it made up special there," Hal said. I could hear my mother saying, "Why doesn't he buy his coffee at the A & P like everyone else!" I wanted very much at that moment to get my mother's voice out of my head. But I replied to her, "Because some of us discover dusty Italian grocery stores in obscure places and it makes life more interesting." As so often in the past, though, she had the last word, "What a waste of time! When does he go to work? Coffee is coffee."

Coffee is not coffee, Ma! This is super-powerful coffee! Wow. As I drank it, everything changed inside me. As everything changed inside me, everything changed outside me, too. Then I had to reconsider everything I'd asked myself about Hal and revise all my opinions. Now what had seemed precious and affected, seemed a valid way to make life better. This coffee stimulated my senses and… How many sensuous experiences had I missed in life. I'd been trained to turn away from sunsets, perfumes, classical music *(la fille aux cheveux de lin)* cuisine… Cuisine! Where had I picked that up. A few hours ago I wouldn't have dared to use the word. Hey, Ma! Cuisine! Mashed potatoes and frozen peas are not cuisine!

"I admire your puppets," I said, though the truth was I did and I didn't. "I wish I had talent."

"Maybe you have talents you haven't discovered yet. What do you like to do?"

"I like to read. And I write in a notebook."

"Well, maybe you'll be a writer."

"I have no education."

"Get some. It's all around you."

"And I don't have the tuition money. I don't even know how you get into a college. How do you apply?"

He laughed and shook his head. "I didn't mean you had to enroll in a college. All I meant was, you should open your eyes."

"Well, but... They're opening."

"Keep them open. Keep your mind open."

7:20 A.M. We went back into Hal's room. He gave me a jacket. "I love that 'schmatte'—that rag—you wear. I really do. But wear this jacket to the army base, please. Also, I want to give you something as a gift. I want to give you something of mine." It was blue and looked like a jacket a cadet would wear. I put it on. It fit perfectly.

Then we lay on the bed and kissed for a while. It wasn't the same. Something had changed. Our spirits were awake and were eyeing each other warily. Sex is fun, honey, but when you wake the spirits, watch out! Who is this guy who's come into my life so recently? What's he want? He's going to change everything. He's already changed everything. I wish he'd go away. I don't want him to go away. I want to be free. I want to be held. I'm scared. I'm happy. I want it to end. I want out. I want it to last forever.

"We don't have time," he said. "But this is so nice. So nice."

He was right. There was no time. We didn't have sex. But what we had was nice. Real nice.

8:05 A.M. He drove me to the army base. Traffic was heavy. He had put the top up. It had begun to rain. Stalled in traffic, we talked. He told a joke. "Two Beacon Hill ladies were walking on The Common. A queen walks by and one lady says to the other, 'Do you know what that is? That's a faggot. And do you know something else? I've been told there's another one in New York, too.' It reminds me of you, last night, at the park."

"Well, I know there are more than two of them now, Hal. There are three, you, me and Morris. And I need another one of your language lessons. What do you call your relationship with Morris? 'Friend?' 'Companion?' 'Husband?' 'Wife?' What?"

"Sex partner," Hal answered.

"But there's more to it than that. I thought he was in love with you."

"If he's in love with me, he's never discussed it with me. Anyway, what's love? Do you think we sit around and talk about love all the time? I'm not sure I believe in love anyway. Morris thinks he's in love with that violinist and he's not happy. I'm only in the market for something that makes me happy. It doesn't seem to me that love makes people happy."

"I thought sex and love went together."

"They don't. Well, I mean... Well, they do, but... You know, Steve, you're very good at what you do, but you should know that that intensity of yours will scare off half the willing men in the world. Do you know what I mean? You put so much into it."

"I thought that was what I was supposed to do!"

"Yes, last night it was the right thing to do. But... They'll want you to be more relaxed about it, more casual. See, that kind of energy, that kind of... And your repertoire is limited. They'll want you to do more. I mean, physically. There's more."

"I'm ready to do more. Any time." I said it defiantly. I wasn't going to be put down. "But I want to do it with you." I knew I shouldn't have said that. I was just setting myself up, to be knocked down. But it was true. So I said it.

Hal just said, "Oh." Just "Oh." But it said it all. Oh, shit, if we only had time! Oh, Steve, it's sweet, but it's over. Oh, if we only didn't have to get so fucked up in Realities. Oh. He reached over and put his hand over my hand. He kept it there for a long time. Then he had to put it back on the steering wheel. Early morning rush hour traffic was so terrible. You have to keep both hands on the wheel. It was the rain. The whole city was paralyzed by the rain.

8:50 A.M. He drove up to the army base and parked outside the gate, where about fifty guys were standing around in the rain waiting to go inside. The pier on which the building had been constructed extended out over the water. The Atlantic had never looked colder and grayer than it did in that rain. The waves lapped at the pilings. There were the usual gulls. I'd hoped Hal would park a few blocks away, but he rolled right up to the gate. He did it because it was raining and why should I get wet? I was thinking of something else. In the movies, the guy that comes for his physical exam in a sports car always has a peroxide blonde beside him. He's a gambler. She's a whore with a heart of gold. Or a chorus girl. Or rich bitch. Well, my life was no movie, and if I waited for Hollywood to film the facts of my life, I'd wait a long time, wouldn't I? I was ashamed of myself for being ashamed. I was being driven up to the gate by a man. Since the gate was closed, we sat there talking. Did the other men look in at us and wonder?

"I'm not rich," Hal said, continuing a conversation we'd been having earlier.

"How much does your father earn?"

"My guess is, fifty thousand a year."

"That's rich."

"No, that's 'comfortable.' Anyway, I'm not my father. I'll be earning about three thousand at the country day school."

"How much will I get in the army?"

"Sixty dollars a month." He'd been there. "If you go in."

"What? I'm here!"

"Yes. Right." He leaned over and opened my door. "Steve. You call me as soon as this is over. I'll be right by the phone. Promise? Oh, Steve, look at those men. Fifty or sixty of the sexiest men in Boston. I want you to have sex with every single one of them!" He laughed, looking at me. I blushed. I couldn't help it. What a way to go into the army!

A man in uniform opened the gate and we walked down the pier toward the building. It took me less than five minutes to find a buddy, an Irish immigrant with no front teeth who told me he'd been in the country six months and was going into the army because he wanted his citizenship. He said he was a carpenter. His name was Jim. Finding a buddy was something I did automatically. You had to blend in. You couldn't make it alone either. You needed a buddy. I realized right away that the army was one big adolescent gang, one more way of opting out for a few more years of hanging out in front of the drugstore watching the broads go by. It wasn't threatening. It was just A Street on a national level. Hang out and don't make waves. Do what you're told, keep your mouth shut, don't do anything that will make you appear to stand out. Don't be different. Just be one of the guys. And have a buddy. But as human beings, we are all unique! I'm unique! Hal's unique! I'm not just a thing. I'm a… spiritual entity! Tell that to the Marines!

Jim. Jim Kiernan. From Roscommon in County Connacht. Red hair, freckled skin, square jaw, big chest, big hands. No front teeth. Where had he lost them? In a fight? Outside a pub? What were the pubs like in Roscommon? Who had hit him and why? Would the army give him a partial plate? The answer was yes. What did it feel like to be a carpenter? How much did he earn? What was his union like? Was he married? No. But very straight! And therefore, very safe. Perfect protective coloration for me. And I could never imagine having sex with Jim. So I was safe there, too. Jim was unique, though. Jim had his own story to tell, too. He'd never hear mine. I'd have to make one up for him. I'd have to invent one. Starting when? How about now?

We got into the building and stood around for a while. We were going to be asked to undress. A doctor was going to cup my balls in his hand and ask me to cough. I should tell him where those balls were last night. No, before they asked us to undress, there'd be a form to fill out. A man came up and barked at us. We moved forward. Jim stayed beside me. Good buddy. This was like summer camp. I was sure glad Jim was there. The army base opened up around us—a factory designed for one purpose, to process unique human beings, to transform them into standardized packages of American cheese. I flowed along with the others. What else could I do? Someone was directing us, but I couldn't see him, couldn't hear him if he was speaking. This wasn't my body. Already, because I was lost in the mass, I had no body. My mind began to go silent. It was better that way. *La fille aux cheveux de lin...* Turn off that music in your mind. O.K. It's off. Wipe that smile off your face, buddy! O.K., it's off, sir. There's still some music in you! I can hear it in your bones. O.K., it's out of my bones! I hear it in your cells! I can't get it out of my cells, sir! Then it's the stockade for you, Private Riley! *La fille. Aux cheveux. De Lin.* The Girl, With the. Flaxen Hair. I liked the very last note of that piece best of all. That note had hovered there last night, hushed and expectant, just before I kissed Hal's cock.

9:35 A.M. The Form! It arrived. "Form," "formality," "a mere formality." As in, "Fill it out automatically without thinking about it." But I had to think about it. That's what my life's about. I have to think about things. Where was The Big Question? I had expected it to be on page one because, for me, it was the only question. And here were lists and lists...! Bed wetting? Bad dreams? Night sweats? Tuberculosis? Rheumatic fever? That had saved Brian. If you'd had a disease, you were safe. They didn't want you. Malaria? Where was it? I couldn't find it. I began to panic. Maybe it wasn't even on here. Maybe it had all been a myth. Measles? Chicken pox? Where! I could feel my heart beating in my chest.

It was the last item. HOMOSEXUAL TENDENCIES. Answer yes or no. Take every second of your life since conception, every word spoken, every moment of love and sex and life, every wink, every blink, every beat. Distill it down to Government Issue. Then answer yes or no. Take Ro and Ralph and Luanne and Hal and reduce them to one single, unidentifiable dot on a page. Then answer yes or no. Take loneliness and longing and anger and ecstasy. Tell us none of it was worth shit. Convince yourself. Then answer yes or no. Because then we will own you. And we know you want to be owned. We know you want to belong. We know you want our approval. And if that's not enough, if you answer yes, we

140

will punish you. You will never get a job. You will be reduced to begging in the streets. And you'll deserve it, because you admitted it. You dared to admit it to us! You are queer! And we'll get you for it. You can count on that.

I couldn't answer it. I couldn't make the mark. I just sat there, staring at the words. HOMOSEXUAL TENDENCIES. Two words. What did they mean? Who had put them there? And why were they there? I saw a guy come out of a room. He began to collect the forms. Could I refuse to answer the question, leave the space blank? That was evasive. That was cowardly. That was a real failure of commitment on my part. Besides, if I left it blank, well, they'd just take me in a room and ask me why it was blank. Then I'd have to make a commitment with a lot of stony-faced army types staring at me. So that wasn't the thing to do. I looked around. A lot of guys hadn't finished yet. A lot of them probably couldn't read it, didn't understand the words! For this one, for instance! What could HOMOSEXUAL TENDENCIES mean to anyone who wasn't gay? Oh, no! They knew. The taunting and mocking and the beatings and the jokes had been going on since grade school. "I'm not one of them!" So, if you could say that, this final question was easy for you.

I was paralyzed. My whole body had turned to stone. Was I going to be the last guy to hand in my form? I was fighting a feeling of anger. But why fight it? Why not just ball up this form and throw it in the man's face? Because then how do you exit? How do you get out of this building? Before I could get to the gate, they'd have restrained me. Then what? No, there was no way out. Anyway, I was angry at myself for letting myself be manipulated into this position by Tim and my mother and everyone else in the world who never asked me who I was or what I was, who just saw me as meat to be packaged and sold to the government. But it was my fault. Why hadn't I ever stood up to them and said, "Fuck you! Fuck you, world! I AM!"

The guy was there, standing in front of me. He was looking down. He could read the question I couldn't answer. He knew. Did he care? Of course not. He picked up thousands of these forms every day of the week. The only person it mattered to was me. Then that "me" inside myself spoke, that voice I sometimes heard in dreams, that spirit figure I'd seen on the edge of sleep. I felt my body tingle. I felt it come alive. It was like my cells filled with light. "Fill it in, Stevie," the voice said. "Enough of this shit!" I marked YES and handed the form to the guy. A big smile broke out on my face. But I wanted to cry, too. I hovered there in my spirit between laughing and crying. It was like being born. The guy took my form, looked at it, and put it under his right arm. The other forms were in his hand. This is how you got cut out of the herd. He went back into the room he'd stepped out of a few minutes before. I saw the door close behind him. A few seconds later it opened again. He looked out and called my name. "Riley. Riley, Steve."

10:05 A.M. I sat facing a man in civilian clothes who was reading to me from a written statement I was going to be asked to sign. I heard him say, "Your homosexual tendencies would make it difficult for you to perform your military service effectively. Is that correct, Mr. Riley? The answer is 'Yes.' I'm going to ask you to sign your name here, please."

I signed it.

"This does not imply that you have ever had a homosexual experience. It simply means that you recognize the existence of homosexual tendencies within yourself which would make it difficult for you to perform your military duties. There is no malfeasance. You are free to leave."

"And my classification?"

"Deferred. No reason stated."

11:20 A.M. I walked to a Shamrock Bar on Summer Street. It was raining heavily. It was a beautiful rain. I enjoyed walking through it. I had three phone calls to make from the bar. As I dialed my home number, my eye caught a headline in the paper being read by the bartender: LANIEL REPORTS FALL OF DIEN-BIENPHU. What was that all about? My mother answered. She sounded very tired. Part of me hated handing any more grief to her. But another part knew it was my life now. It no longer had anything to do with her. I think she knew it, too. I said, "I'm in a bar a couple of blocks from the army base. I failed my physical."

There was a long silence. Then she said, "Well, you come on home, Stevie. These things happen. We'll work it out. We've worked things out in the past."

"Sure," I said. "We're survivors."

Then I called Luanne. I said, "I'll need that indispensible item now. I told them the truth. I'm not going into the army after all."

"Oh, honey! You did it! You told them. I never thought you would."

"Yes, I told them. So I'll come by later to pick up that bedroll." Because I was going on the road. It gets cold out there and you need a bedroll. It's indispensible.

"Steve, there's nothing out there except terrible places like Columbus and Omaha and Saint Louis. They are absolutely awful places. Please don't go."

"They couldn't be any more awful than Boston."

"But they are! Believe me. I've been there. Why do you think I came to Boston if it wasn't to get away from terrible places like that."

The bartender laid the paper on the bar and went off to serve a customer. I looked down. "...No information on de Castries and survivors. Final report tells of lack of ammunition, hand-to-hand fighting, says 'We will not surrender!'" I picked up on a funny feeling among the men in the bar. They were strangely excited and were talking together in an animated way. Something was up! What was it?

Luanne said, "Steve, you fooled me. I didn't think I could be fooled, but you fooled me. When you pick up your bedroll, pick up your friend's guitar, too. He left it here last night. Steve, I will never believe that you're that way. Never! I don't care what you say, I know better."

A wiry, dark-haired man with wildly excited eyes was ordering drinks for the house. The bartender put a bottle of beer beside me. The men were talking about the fall of a Fort in French Indochina. Where was that? By buying me a beer, the man was including me in whatever was going on in here. A warning buzzer went off in my brain. Be careful!

"Luanne, what can I say? Things happen. We toss a coin and there we are, up to our necks in it. But what can we do? We do the best we can. Then we move on."

"Oh, Steve," she said.

Then I called Hal. He might have reconsidered. He might not even answer the phone. Or if he answered, he might say he didn't want to get involved. I'd come on real loving and tender with him and it had scared him. I didn't really expect him to answer. But then, once he did answer, I knew I'd known absolutely in my spirit all along that he would answer.

"I told the truth, Hal," I said.

"How do you feel about it?" he asked.

"Clean. Cleansed. Like Ivory Soap."

"Where are you now?"

"In a Shamrock Bar on Summer Street."

"I'll be there as soon as I can. I'm leaving the house right now."

I hung up the phone. The wiry, excited man was right there in my face. He was drunk. "They had no ammunition left. They fought them off with bed posts. There was no water. They couldn't get the wounded out. Think of that. The suffering." The excitement in this man! It reminded me of something. It was like sex. Men like this waited all their lives for wars to begin and then acted like this. He was crazy. All the men in this bar were crazy. A war had started somewhere, so they'd gone out of their minds! And Hal was going to walk into the middle of this madness. I called again to tell him I'd meet him somewhere else. There was no answer. He was already on his way.

12:20 P.M. My fear was that Hal would walk in carrying an umbrella. I had to focus my fear on something, so I picked that. Hal with an umbrella walking into a group of men who were crazy to go to war. I knew these guys. I grew up with them. These were the ones who stoned synagogues and wrote KILL FAGGOTS on walls. These were the ones who beat you up in parks and playgrounds. Every once in a while the government provided a war for them so that they could kill someone legally. The government bought their bodies, processed them as human meat and shipped them off. Then the bodies were shipped back, mutilated or dead. But they weren't faggots. They were men. Faggots loved. Real men killed.

When Hal came in, he wasn't carrying an umbrella. When I looked at his face, I forgot about umbrellas. His face was eager, open, trusting, expectant. All that. Vulnerable, too, of course. We're so vulnerable when we allow ourselves to feel that way. Susceptible to pain, yes. Open to it. But why not? Close yourself off and you die inside, right? So why not let yourself love? He saw me sitting there at the bar and came over. "Is that a pistol in your pocket? Or are you just happy to see me?" He had rain in his hair. Later on, outside, in a safer place, I'd reach up and brush it away.

We got out of there. We walked through the rain toward the car. I told him I was leaving Boston. "I want to be free. I'm just going to walk away," I said. "I'm just going to keep walking. I'll find a place. There's got to be a better place than Boston."

"Hitchhiking isn't free, Steve. It's the least 'free' thing in the world. You're totally dependent on other people for rides. And once you get in someone's car, you have to go where they go. You're trapped."

He was right! So much for my plan.

"Besides, it rains out there. You stand by the side of the road and get rained on. You might as well stay here. Here, if it rains, you can duck inside. See?"

"Hal, you just destroyed my whole dream!"

"Hang around a while. Morris doesn't really want to leave Boston. He's all hung up on that violinist. You could drive across the country with me. I didn't want to go with Morris anyway. He's such a kvetch. He's the world's worst backseat driver. Yatta, yatta, all the way across the country. Of course I'm going to have to lie to him. If he ever found out I didn't want him to go, nothing would keep him out of that bucket seat. Anyway, once we get there, you and I can go our separate ways if we want to."

"What's 'kvetch' mean?"

"Nagging bitch. A whiner. A constant complainer."

"Teach me some more words."

"'Bubeleh.' That's you."

"It means something nice, right? I can tell from the way you say it. What's it mean?"

"I can't tell you out here on a public street. Later, in private."

"It sounds nice, driving across the country with you. But I can't. I don't know how to drive. I don't have a license." Did I have any other dreams floating around to be shot down?

"Well, I'll teach you. Once we get into Ohio, the roads just run straight for a thousand miles. I'll give you the wheel and all you need to do is steer. Besides, you'll have a licensed driver, me, beside you."

"What's it like in California?" I asked.

"You'll see," he said.

BOOKS AVAILABLE FROM AMETHYST PRESS

IDOLS
By Dennis Cooper $8.95

BEDROOMS HAVE WINDOWS
By Kevin Killian $8.95

HORSE
By Bo Huston $8.95

These books are available from your favorite bookseller or by mail from:

Amethyst Press
462 Broadway—Suite 4000
New York, NY 10013

Add $1.50 postage and handling for one book. For more than one book add 10% of order total. New York City residents please add 8% sales tax. US currency only.

John Gilgun was born in 1935 in Malden, Massachusetts. His poems and stories have appeared in *The James White Review, Paragraph I,* and *On the Line* (Crossing Press). His previous book, *Everything That Has Been Shall Be Again* (Bieler Press, 1981) won four awards. This is his first published novel. He lives in San Francisco.